African Roar

An Eclectic Anthology of African Authors

Edited by

Emmanuel Sigauke

&

Ivor W. Hartmann

A

StoryTime

Publication

Cover design by Ivor W. Hartmann

ISBN: 978-0-620-47463-4

Contents

Foreword

There is no doubt that the internet, together with digital publishing, has changed – and is still changing – the world of published literature. In the case of Africa and the African Diaspora, I certainly believe it has been for the better. Never before have so many African writers been visibly active and prolific. There is a revolution going on in the world of African literature, an *African Roar* that is beginning to echo around the world.

When I first started *StoryTime* in 2007, it was because I saw there was a need to provide an independent global online platform for new and established African writers, a platform where all fiction genres were accepted and the only requirement was a good story well told. From the very beginning I had a dream of utilising *StoryTime* to build up a body of work from all over Africa and the African Diaspora, from which eventually a book anthology might be drawn. At last that dream has been realised, and could not have been possible without the enthusiasm and support of all the *StoryTime* authors. One of the authors, Emmanuel Sigauke, offered to co-edit *African Roar* with me back when it was still just a dream.

African Roar is to be the first in an annual anthology series that will continue to select the very best of what has been published in the *StoryTime* ezine throughout the preceding year. The story selections were made through a process of a public voting by the *StoryTime* readers and then a final editors' selection. Each story then went through a rigorous editing process to ensure its highest potential.

What we have arrayed in this first anthology is an outstanding body of fiction from some of the finest emerging African writers today. With authors from all over Africa and in the African Diaspora, *African Roar* is now and promises to be a true cross-section of African literature. However, the proof is in the reading and I hope you enjoy this small banquet of African literature as much as we have in preparing it for you.

   – **Ivor W. Hartmann**.

I have been honoured to co-edit this rich anthology of fiction. Working with Ivor W. Hartmann, one of the most efficient editors on the African continent, was a great experience. We communicated with each other and with the writers, one email at a time, sent drafts back and forth, as each day drew us closer to the reality of the book you are holding. Reading the submissions, I was constantly reminded of the magnitude of creative talent that the writers displayed through their works. Then to think that this was just the beginning of a continent-wide initiative turned out, in my thinking, to be no small matter. The imaginations that produced this work are fertile, and if in the short time *StoryTime* has existed it could produce this much work and attract the number of writers displayed on its website and in this volume, I can just imagine what will have happened in two, three, or four years. This new outlet for African writers comes with the promise of providing unique fiction to the reader, unique not only because it is by African writers, but also because these are writers whose talents may not have been discovered this early. I am satisfied with the state of writing in Africa and I can confidently say that now — this decade, this century — is the time for the world to discover the full potential of the continent's literary might.

The stories in *African Roar* showcase some of the best emerging African writers on the continent and abroad. Originally published online, these stories bear testimony to the importance of the World Wide Web as a creative outlet and resource for contemporary African writers. Of great significance is the range of issues these writers portray and

Foreword

the wide spectrum of authors from different African countries. This is matched by the growing world demand for African writing, in part enabled by the internet as an information vehicle and a marketing tool. Ivor W. Hartmann has already said it, but it is worth restating here: *African Roar* is the first book in a series that is bound to revolutionise the African short story.

Here we have writers of great promise: Novuyo Rosa Tshuma with her 'Big Pieces, Little Pieces', where the narrator remembers the death of her mother at the hands of her abusive father and the horrors of a patriarchal world order; Kola Tubosun's fast-paced story of a man who musters the courage to face the unknown in an HIV/AIDS-testing; Masimba Musodza's 'Yesterday's Dog', which links two disturbing historical periods in Zimbabwe, a story whose rendering is as dizzying as it is engaging; Ayodele Morocco-Clarke's 'The Nestbury Tree', which shows the dangers of superstition and misdirected faith; Chris Mlalazi's 'A Cicada in the Shimmer', a story that recalls Jorge Luis Borges, with a shot of Kafka — the enchanting weaving of details infused with the blurred reality of an uneven Zimbabwe; Beaven Tapureta's 'Cost of Courage', dreamy and dazzling, presenting a narrator who guides us through the horrifying landscape of the Harare ghetto, where dreams die before they sprout; Ivor W. Hartmann's 'Lost Love', which shows us that once lost, love is hard to find, but its memories may just as well pass as a new kind of love; Chuma Nwokolo's enthralling story-telling in 'Quarterback & Co.', whose protagonist will reveal the evils of greed and corporate profiteering; Nana A. Damoah's 'Truth Floats', a portrayal of friendship, love and betrayal ; and Ayesha Harruna Attah's 'Tamale Blues', a beautiful tale that will leave the reader asking for more. Like the protagonist in 'Tamale Blues', we will be left "looking at the tall, blue grass", anticipating the next roar.

– **Emmanuel Sigauke**.

African Roar

Big Pieces, Little Pieces

Novuyo Rosa Tshuma

Father was very particular about his belongings. Take the time when Mama burnt his Che Guevara shirt, the frayed one with a black and white man who looked like somebody called Bob Marley but without his dreadlocks. You had always thought that shirt was a sweaty-smelly thing because Father wore it only when he went to some place called 'Jim' which made him sweaty-smelly. But the way he smashed Mama's Philips iron against the wall and screamed *what kind of nincompoop destroyed something so revolutionary*, made that shirt as good as new. Ever since then Mama had always tried the iron on a cloth first, then carefully pressed his clothes, hesitantly, as though she expected at any moment the smell of roasted fabric to waft to her nostrils.

And the time Jabu spilled dye on his trousers. The way Father cupped Jabu's face and gave him a double clap left your ears ringing and it felt as though it was you he had clapped and not Jabu. When he was gone, you hugged Jabu and you both cried and you told him it was going to be all right. Later, when the bruise at the nape of his neck was just a black patch, you laughed at him and asked him what he had been trying to do, stealing Mama's dye. Didn't he know that Jesus didn't like children stealing? That was when he stuck his tongue out and told you that Jesus was just some story made up to colonise black people's traditions.

"You don't even know what the word 'colonise' means," you said.

"Oh yes I do!" he shot back.

"Really? What does it mean?"

He began to stammer, the way he always did when he was lying or nervous or guilty, and you laughed. That was how Jabu always got caught.

"Do *you* know what it means?" he asked finally.

"Yes I do," you replied, giving him that what-do-you-expect look.

"What does it mean?"

"I don't want to tell you."

"Ha! There, you don't know!"

"Yes I do!"

"No you don't!"

"Yes I do! I just don't want to tell you."

"Well, Father said it so it's true, so there!"

You couldn't argue with that, so you pushed Jabu and told him again how stupid he had been to steal Mama's dye.

Auntie Tshitshi had said never to argue with Father, he was the head of the family and knew what was best for everyone. Mama had stood up then, lifted her dress and petticoat to show Auntie Tshitshi the blistering red stripes on her thighs.

"Is this what is best for me, eh?" she screamed, tears running down her cheeks. "Answer me! Eh, I ask you, is this what is best for me!"

Auntie Tshitshi looked away and chided Mama for being such a cry baby. "Baba used to beat Mama up and she took it like a woman. It's a good sign, *sis' wakhe*, it shows that he loves you. Look, he disciplines the children, why, because he loves them. *Lo yiwo umendo sis' wakhe.*"

Big Pieces, Little Pieces

"So this is married life," Mama repeated, shaking her head. "Well, I am thinking that if this is married life then I must take the children and return to my people."

Auntie Tshitshi threw her hands in the air. "Heh! You forget, don't you, Grace, the cattle that shrivelled up our herds and fattened yours when you came into this house! You forget your bride price! If you want to shame your people go ahead, but my brother's seeds shall remain where you bore them, right here, in this house." She stood up and stomped her feet on the carpet.

"Sisi, please, you are his sister, he may not listen to me but maybe he will listen to you, talk to him, please, tell him to stop this…" Again she raised her dress "…before he kills us all." Mama held out her hands.

Auntie Tshitshi snickered. "I have never seen such a woman, honestly! Is it my fault that you do not know how to appease your husband, that you anger him all the time? I will say it again, *lo yiwo umendo.*"

That was when Mama saw you leaning against the doorframe. She wiped her tears abruptly and ordered you to fetch a glass of water for Auntie Tshitshi.

You only wished Mama wasn't so careless, that she didn't make Father so angry all the time. Mama was wasteful, Father always said. People who did not go to work did not appreciate the cost of things, the way he did. You remember he said this sadly, swinging the knobkerrie in his hand as Mama tried to gather the broken glass bowl from the floor. That was when Mama said quietly that it wasn't her fault that Mrs. Sibanda had called them in because you drew those pictures.

"After all, you teach your children to tell the truth. Let them speak the truth."

You began to tremble because you knew that Mama had said too much. Father clutched the knobkerrie so tight that his knuckles shone. His face seemed to be swelling, swelling like it would burst. Any moment now he would do his tantrums. The fist of the knobkerrie would land on Mama in dull thuds, dig black bruises into her skin.

He grabbed the pot on the stove, the huge black one that Mama used to boil water on the coal stove whenever ZESA cut the power and the lights went out. You heard Jabu's wee-wee splashing on the floor before the water hit Mama. She was doubled over with the glass bowl pieces wrapped in newspaper in her hand, her face tilted towards Father, her eyes wild. The fan sputtering overhead seemed to be spinning very fast now, making your head spin fast too. Mama's scream made your head spin faster than the whirring blades. It screeched in your ears long after it was gone, diluted the angry *whrr-whrr* of the blades so that you thought your head was bursting, and haunted you for many months after that. The kitchen was falling. The walls were coming at you. Her cheeks were peeling off, exposing the white inner flesh, the skin peeling off the way skin peels off from potatoes just after you boil them. Jabu buried his face in your neck and you put your arms around him and held on tight.

You wished you hadn't drawn those pictures, the ones of Mama and Father. Maybe then Mrs. Sibanda wouldn't have frowned the way she did, called Miss Greene to come and see the pictures and later, Mama and Father. And maybe if Mama hadn't dropped the glass bowl Father wouldn't have burnt her with the water.

And so the day you dropped Father's beer mug you felt the world stop. He had told you hadn't he, to leave it in the sink, but Mama had made him do his tantrums again and you thought you would do something to make him smile. You climbed the chair and put the mug under running water. You marvelled at the way the water made the mug shine. It was so big, made of heavy glass that weighed a tonne in your chubby hands. You ran the soap lovingly over it, your fingers lingering on the bright red label that read 'CASTLE LAGER'.

Big Pieces, Little Pieces

You'd seen the label many times on Father's beer bottles. You were always careful to watch Father. You knew that he drank *Ingwebu* more than any other beer, but whenever the Patterson's came for a visit, Mama would rinse the little glasses and Father would take out the bottle of Jack Daniel's. You frowned when you remembered that even Mrs. Patterson drank Jack Daniel's. It wasn't right for a woman to drink. Father had said so. You remember he had been unbuckling his belt as he said so, asking Mama if she thought it was proper for a woman to drink. Mama slowly went down on her knees, saying over and over that she was sorry.

"Do you think it's proper for a woman to drink?"

"Please Baba, please, you saw how Christine kept shoving the glass to my lips-"

"If a woman must drink, what must a man do now, eh? Is she a man now, eh, that she must drink?"

"No no please but you said I could take a sip-"

"So it's my fault now eh, that you are loose heh?"

"No no please please-"

Down the belt went.

"Do you want to be like that stupid woman, eh!"

Like a whip,

"Tottering all over the place like a whore!"

The way you'd seen the cattle boys crack their whips on the donkeys' backs whenever they pulled the cart too slowly.

"Next you'll be wearing trousers in my house like those shebeen whores, eh!"

Mama didn't go to the doctor. You hid behind the doors and watched as she limped all over the house, a wrapper bunched up around her legs, whiplashes of dry tears zigzagging down her cheeks. And Father was nice after that, the way he always was after he did his tantrums. He brought Mama presents wrapped in nice paper, shiny glittery material with balloon decorations that you would take afterwards to make wedding dresses for your Barbie doll.

"It's your fault," he said over and over. "You shouldn't make me so angry."

Mama said nothing.

"I'm sorry."

She took the present and still said nothing.

"I love you."

But she did not smile. She dragged her feet wherever she went. You wished she would smile, wished she would sweep the courtyard with a spring to her step, the way she used to. The house was heavy when she did not smile. She made Father do his tantrums more when she did not smile.

You stood in the shadows of the hall way and watched as she cried, sniffling into the phone over and over that she could not go to the doctor, because this time he wouldn't believe her if she said she had fallen down the stairs.

So, you were rinsing the mug and thinking how proud of you Father would be. You should have placed it on the sink then got off the chair, you knew you should have. Instead, you tucked it in the nook of your little arm, thinking how heavy it was and how strong you were, gripped the chair and began to climb down. You felt it slip from your arm, you felt it and your limbs fought with the air. It seemed to fall in the slowest of motion. Then *kpa!*, the deafening crash and the pieces were skidding across Mama's tiles, big pieces and little pieces. All you could think of as you got off the chair were Father's burnt shirt and dyed trousers. You were crying as you tried to gather the pieces. You thought if you gathered them all, you would piece Father's beer mug back together. You didn't hear his footsteps, but you saw him there, his huge sandaled feet by the doorway.

You wanted to say sorry but the snot kept choking you, bubbling from your nostrils and popping like little balloons. When you saw the blood on your hands you screamed. It wasn't so much the pain of the shards digging into your skin as it was the sight of the blood that made you scream. It was just like the blood on Mama's sarong, the day Father kicked her and she lost the baby.

You knew the blows were coming. Father was screaming and you were screaming, then Mama was screaming. You were trying to say sorry, you would find every piece and stick them back together, please. But Father kept on pummelling you, kicking and yelling and swearing.

"You stupid. Your fault. Stupid like your mother. Stupid. *You stupid!*"

Sharp pain burned you wherever his blows landed.

You saw Mama rushing towards you. Father struck her and she seemed to be flying, flying right across the room. Her head hit the corner of the coal stove and she fell face down, a sick *crack crack* with each bounce. You could no longer see her, but the blood was following the lines of the tiles, crawling towards you. You screamed but you didn't, because no sound came from your mouth. Jabu's wee-wee reached your lips before the blood did, warm against your tongue. Then you tasted Mama's blood, salty blood that made you want to vomit.

The cemetery is an ugly place for the Jacaranda. You used to associate the Jacaranda with happy times, happy places, because you thought the purple bloom of its leaves in October was such a beautiful colour, better even than the trees with the reddish-orange leaves. Your road is littered with them. There is a huge one next to your gate; its branches are spread out like an umbrella. It used to be nice, pressing your face against the window in Father's car, taking in the purple blur as you drove past a string of them. You remember how Khulu Mlambo never came to the city when the jacarandas were in bloom because they made his eyes watery and his nose run. But he is here now.

You hate the Jacaranda, ever since the morning you saw the Waneka Bird. You heard it warbling beneath the

African Roar

Jacaranda Tree by your window, squatting over the jagged pieces of its eggs. Its red fluffy chest was puffed up, the way Jabu's jaws swelled when he had mumps. It darted about its eggshells, the yolk glazing the purple confetti, flapping its black wings. Its cry was mournful, and when you squinted you thought you saw the glint of jewels in its coal black eyes. It warbled and warbled, pecking the eggshells. When it was gone you ran out into the cool morning air. The grass wiped its dew onto your feet, making your *patapatas* muddy. You crouched over the broken eggs, and you felt sorry for the Waneka Bird. Its nest sat skewed on a branch overhead, now empty. You wondered if it had been a Daddy Waneka Bird or a Mummy Waneka Bird, and if the Daddy would beat the Mummy up for the broken eggs. Now you wish you had never touched those broken eggs, surely they were bad luck, because later that day you broke Father's beer mug.

The man who drove you to the cemetery has a nose just like Father's. It used to be such fun, sitting cross-legged in front of Father's sofa, clamping your hand over your mouth so he wouldn't hear your giggles when he began to snore because it was funny the way his nostrils blared open each time he snored. You used to stare in wonder at that nose that used to fill up Father's face, squint at the tufts of hair peeking from those blaring nostrils, and worry that if they continued to grow, they would block Father's nose.

You miss the happy days, the time when Father would sweep you into his arms. It always felt like flying, swinging in those arms. Even when Father made as if to let go, you never feared, because those strong arms felt so safe. You would place your little hands on that wide face, place them on Father's cheeks, and marvel at the leathery feel, the contours that appeared when he smiled. You would look deep into those kola nut laughing eyes, see yourself in them, and begin to chuckle. Round and round you would go, the ribbons in your hair fluttering over your face, the

Big Pieces, Little Pieces

wind lifting your dress and whooshing around your legs and tickling your heart. Then he would put you down and it would be Jabu's turn.

Mama's grave is so small. The flowers have shrivelled up and turned an ugly ashy brown. You place your bunch on the mound. The rose is the most beautiful, you think, just like Mama. It's blushing, the way Mama used to blush whenever Father would tell her how beautiful she was, how her skin made him think of bathing in a stream of coconut milk. The way Jabu blushes whenever anyone pinches his cheeks and smiles that smile that tells him to smile back and fusses over what a pretty boy he is.

It was raining the day they buried Mama. Thick heavy sheets, Jabu says, that soaked him despite the umbrella. It was the same day when the doctor came with the bad men. The same men who came to talk to Father when the Factory Manager reported him, you could tell from their ugly brown uniforms, the shiny badges on their jackets. The government had almost taken Father's business license then. You had felt sorry for the government; didn't they know that if they made Father angry he would do his tantrums, beat them up the way he beat the Factory Manager up for reporting him?

You thought the doctor was such a nice man, the way he brought you sweets when he came with the bad men. Auntie Tshitshi told you not to tell them anything, she grabbed your hand and said the doctor was bringing bad people to talk to you, that you must say absolutely nothing to them. You nodded vigorously so she would stop squeezing your hand so hard.

You didn't want to say anything, you really didn't, but the doctor was so nice, he gave you a sweet and smiled so nicely and asked you what had happened.

First, you said you fell down the stairs. One of the bad men was scribbling furiously on a note pad, the fat one with the wart on his face. When the doctor persisted you asked for your lawyer, the way you'd seen them do on those American movies. He laughed and gave you another sweet and promised you that everything would be all right, just tell him.

You began to cry.

What happened, what happened, the doctor kept on asking.

You didn't know, please, your head hurt, you wanted to sleep.

Okay, but first, what happened. Don't be afraid. I'm your friend. What happened.

So you told them. Everything.

The Jacaranda is right next to Mama's grave. It is crooked, as if someone has twisted it to one side. You hate the way it has sprinkled its purple leaves on Mama's grave.

You squeeze Jabu's hand. He is trying to be strong, you can tell. Khulu Mlambo chided him for crying on your way to the cemetery. He said he must not cry, patted his shoulder and smiled, that old man's smile of his that always made you grimace because you would see the yucky green sappy pieces of the medicinal leaves he is always chewing, dangling from his brown teeth. He smiled and told Jabu to be strong because he had to be a man now, the one who should look after you. You looked at Jabu and wondered if that meant he had to beat you up too.

His face crumbles. You hold him and tell him that everything is going to be all right.

Don't cry. Please don't cry.

You shut your eyes tight and drag the snot back up your nose. Your little face is wet. Because it's all your fault. Mama wouldn't have died, and they wouldn't have taken Father away, if only you hadn't dropped that beer mug.

Big Pieces, Little Pieces

Novuyo Rosa Tshuma is a Zimbabwean writer based in South Africa. Her works have been published in print anthologies and online publications. She was the winner of the Intwasa Short Story Competition 2009 and a participant in the Caine Prize Workshop 2010. Her musings may be found at www.novuyorosa.blogspot.com.

African Roar

Behind the Door

Kola Tubosun

Why I finally decided to take the test, I no longer remember. There was no compulsion whatsoever beyond the recurring curiosity that was never strong enough to overcome all reasonable and unreasonable resistance. After about a week in and out of the clinic, getting one immunisation injection or another, the last thing I wanted on my arm was another needle jab. No desire for the certitude of my wholesomeness was enough to goad me into the ordeal of venipuncture, and my thoughts dangled for years between unexplainable reluctance and indifference, until the soft-spoken doctor who had just completed some of my medical forms on this particular day hinted quite casually as she handed back to me a sheaf of papers that I could take the test if I wanted to, if only for my own records. Most of these medical forms, she explained, mandated the patient to take the test as well, and it was a wonder that mine did not. "And you could do it just behind that door."

"Really?"

"Yes," she said, pointing to a closed room. "And you would have the result in less than fifteen minutes."

I was intrigued. The last time I came to this place I had searched all around for the test centre and nobody, not even the nurses, seemed to know where the test took place. That seemed odd. Those few who volunteered to direct me were more curious about why I wanted to do the test than about my sense of urgency and exasperation. They looked at me strangely and asked politely whether I was sick, or whether I had been referred by a trained physician. In the end, they still gave me wrong directions, and I left, dissatisfied, but glad at least to have made the effort. Maybe it was a sign that I was right not to have done it all this while. Maybe I didn't need to know what was in my blood. Maybe ignorance is bliss after all, but the fact that I could know my status within minutes in the closed room with no label except a bold letter "9" intrigued me beyond reason, so I hopped in there. There was someone already in with the female phlebotomist when I entered. It was a young man of around my age who was getting pre-test counselling. I couldn't tell by the look on his face if he was as worried as I was. He surely could not have been able to tell from mine.

"Sit down there," the woman said after we exchanged greetings. She waved me towards one of the iron seats, and then she returned her attention to the other patient.

She summoned him to come closer, and he did. He got up to sit by her at the lab table. As he folded the arms of his shirt in readiness for a needle insertion into his veins, I got immediately apprehensive. I had never liked needles, or tablets, but I liked the needles even less, and I would have done anything to avoid another insertion, about the third in one week. My mind wandered off to a public awareness website of a previous day where I had read that an alternative method of testing exists, involving using the scrapings from the lining of the patient's cheeks instead of their blood. I liked this alternative, and I began to scheme how best to convey my preference to the woman when my turn eventually came.

But then she spoke to him, "I won't be needing your veins, young man", and I was relieved from afar. "For this, all I need is a little drop of blood from your thumb. Roll down your sleeves and let me have your left hand..."

Behind the Door

Even he seemed pleased enough as she went through the quick process of sucking the droplet of blood with a specialized device from the now expanding crimson jot in the middle of his thumb. She placed it immediately on a strip of coloured cardboard slide on the table right in front of her, and said to him: "All we have to do now is wait. Why don't you sit outside for a little while?"

He got up and wiped his thumb with a piece of cotton wool while we exchanged a stoic glance, just before he left the room.

"You may come now," she said to me, smiling. "Sit here."

"Thank you," I replied and sat down.

She pulled out a long notebook where she had written some information about the previous lad and started to copy out some of my personal information from the little crimson paper that I presented to her, which I had got from the nurses outside.

"So you came here to do the test…"

"Yes, of course. I've always wanted to do the test. There's nothing wrong with me."

"Of course, young man. Of course."

"I'm sure you call it Voluntary Testing."

She smiled. "Yes"

I looked around as she wrote, wondering what it must be like to work as a hospital phlebotomist, with the distinction of being able to break both the good and the bad news to numerous visitors. On one of the walls was an enlightening campaign poster about the ills of living a reckless life.

She took another look at me and I smiled back, a little uneasily, not being able to tell what she was thinking until she asked quite amiably if I was indeed ready to take the test. She's a specialist at this, I figured, and she must have been told never to proceed without being sure of the visitor's absolute consent.

"Yes, of course," I said, showing little surprise. I had come by myself after all, well prepared to be asked all sorts of questions. "I'm sure," I continued. "I was here yesterday, looking for this room, but it seemed either that you closed very early, or that there was no one in when I came to the door."

She ignored my last statement and continued, "What do you know about the virus and disease, young man, anyway?"

"I know everything," I said, and she looked up.

"Really?"

"Yes."

"Interesting."

Betraying no further interest in my ramblings beyond the usual humouring necessary to grant such a conceited response, she smiled. Maybe she saw through the shield, and saw in my straight face a barely disguised defence mechanism against sad, unexpected news, or maybe she was just in the mood to indulge in a little mischief of her own. She put the pen down and said: "Why don't you tell me what you know?"

I knew this for sure, that it could be contacted through sex, and anything that involved blood transfusion, be it a wrong pin prick, a razor wound, a clipper, or things like that. I listed them one after the other, and wondered aloud if there were other points that I was already forgetting.

"Okay, so you know, it seems."

"Ah-ha," I continued. "I also know that it has no cure."

"It can be managed," she replied.

"That's what they say."

"That's what they say?"

"Well, yes," I replied. "I mean that's what we hear everywhere these days."

She smiled, but I was curious. So I asked: "What if someone who tests positive begins to take the drugs, how long would they really have to live from then on?"

"That is not a question I could answer," she said. "You know, it depends on a lot of things. I mean if someone who is positive gets into a car now, and then has a fatal accident, and dies, would that be the fault of the virus?"

"Of course not, but I'm sure you understand my question."

"Well, the point I'm making is that the drugs we have now could keep infected people in normal health for as long as they take the drugs correctly and consistently."

"And the drugs are free?"

"Yes, they are, as is this test. Do you have any more questions?"

I shook my head. There were many things going on in my head, no doubt, none of which could immediately manifest as a sensible statement of more than just a tactic of delay.

"So, you are ready for the test then?"

I didn't know if I was, but I said, "Yes."

A little fly buzzed by and I ignored it.

"You do sound so confident, and it could turn out that I find something viral in your blood. What would happen then? Have you thought about it?"

"Well, if that happens do tell me. I think I can take it."

"Tell me, are you a Christian or a Muslim?"

"What?" I asked in mock disbelief.

"Which of them are you?"

Was she trying to confirm that I had sufficient religious background to receive the worst possible outcome? I paused for a second before I said: "I'm none of the above."

"No, seriously," she said. "I have to fill something in this space."

"Okay, just write Christian there then. I don't know what being religious has to do with one's will to live or die. In any case, Islam and Christianity are not the only religions in the country."

"Student or worker?"

"This time I have to say both."

A pause.

"Give me just one."

"But I really am both. I am a university student, but I also work."

"Okay then. Come with me."

I followed her to the lab table and was going to ask her whether she had done the test on herself before, but I decided against it, convinced that she must have, at some point.

"What happens when one tests positive? Do you know?"

Her response confirmed that she had heard this question many times before: "Well, mostly we will just ask you first to do a few more tests to confirm that it is really the virus, before we know what to do next."

"So you are telling me that it's possible that this test shows positive and the other test shows negative?"

Her "yes" came in a firm tone that now made me uneasy. "It has happened before, you know. Sometimes there are some other infections that may manifest themselves on this test, and may not in fact be the virus."

I was surprised, but more than that I was now scared. Not that there was anything really to be scared of, but her latest disclosure was leading me to consider the possibility and consequences of being wrongly diagnosed. I did not like where my riotous thoughts quickly went.

"Let me ask you a last question," I said, after a short pause.

"Alright. You seem really curious."

"What is the rate of infection in this part of the country?"

"Well, it depends on the organisation that did the statistics."

"No. I mean in your hospital. You do this every day, right?"

"Yes."

"Like how many people, on average, come here for testing every day?"

"About twelve."

"Okay. Now about how many of them turn positive?"

"I would say about two."

Behind the Door

"Really?"

"Yes." She was firm.

Oh my God!

"Don't be surprised, good sir. The infection is actually that prevalent. With every ten tests I perform, there's usually one positive person, at least. That is why we encourage people to come out and test themselves. There are actually more infected people roaming the streets than we know."

I did not smile.

"So how many tests have you conducted today?" I asked.

She was busy writing in the notebook, so she gave no response. The statistics are not in my favour if all the people she had tested today were already negative, I thought. I could be the scapegoat. Oh wait, mathematics doesn't work that way. Today may be the exception. Or in any case, the day is still too young for despair. The real unfortunate fella may be walking in very soon to receive his news. It is not for me. But even if this woman had already registered three positive people in her inglorious notebook today, was there anything in the world of random figures that said that I couldn't be another one? Damn, I should have spent more time in the arithmetic classes...

She gave me a wad of cotton wool on one hand, and in a quick movement of a professional punctured my right thumb with the little pin before I could scream for her to stop. She smiled assuredly, and proceeded to transfer the drop of my blood onto the little testing strip of cardboard resting on the table.

"Why don't you go wait outside?"

"For how long?"

"Well, just for a few minutes until the result shows on the strip."

She picked it up, and I saw her apply a drop of some clear transparent liquid to the blood from something similar to an eye dropper, before replacing the strip on the table. I wiped the blood off my thumb and headed towards the door.

"Please call the other guy to come back in."

"Okay."

I stopped to peep at the little strip of paper that held the other guy's blood and tried in vain to decipher what each of the colours that had formed on the strip meant. I discovered nothing, so I headed out, found the young man and told him he was wanted inside.

A few minutes on the hospital bench in the corridor ended up as the longest ones of my life. They were few, but they contained a range of similar thoughts of gloom that circled my throbbing head like vultures around a dying desert traveller. I panicked. And suddenly, the random glances towards me by passers-by suddenly began to carry a new curious significance. How could I have failed to notice that the woman in red shoes giggled for a few seconds before she turned the corner, or that the little boy beside her pointed in my direction and said something to his mother? Random images of a gruesome death competed with my beating heart as twin punches of a ruthless fighter in the fighting ring of my recurring memory, and all my past and future goals were instantly reduced to the now suddenly loud ticking hands of the hospital clock: mis-takes-o-mis-sions-care-less-ness-es-ad-ven-tures-in-dare-de-vil-ry,   a grand conspiracy.

Then suddenly, it was my turn to go back in. The young man had got his result written on his crimson sheet of paper, and his face retained its staid, unrevealing demeanour. I peeped into the sheet he was holding, but I couldn't pick out a word out of his result as much as I tried.

As I closed the door behind me and saw the woman smiling, my heart skipped a beat.

"I hope I passed," I said, softly.

"Let me have your phone number," she replied.

It didn't sound like a good sign.

"So, what was it then?"

Behind the Door

"Don't be too impatient, young man. I saw you singing as you came in. It was as if you already knew your result."

"Well, singing is good for all occasions. I really couldn't help it then."

She told me a story, deepening an already killing suspense: "There was this man that once came here, a long time ago, who, before the test, confessed to having lived a very rough life, if you know what I mean."

"Yes."

"But when I gave him the result of his test, he couldn't believe his eyes. He didn't believe that he could ever be tested negative. He had to look at the result again and again just to be sure."

"That's interesting. I know that I couldn't be positive, I just wanted to be sure."

"Well, it's all there" she said, pointing at the crimson sheet of paper on which she then began to write. "But you should come back in six month's time, you know. Some of these strains take six months to manifest."

"That's encouraging." I thought aloud, and she smiled back at me. "So one is thusly never truly free of the paranoia of the unexpected, isn't it?" I asked.

"Well, the best thing would be to begin to live free of needless risk," she replied, partly cajoling. "You young children of nowadays should at least consider your parents before you take your stupid risks. If you don't consider your lives, you should at least consider theirs."

I laughed. Her tone sounded quite familiar. I looked at her again and I knew that she must be a mother herself. At around her late thirties, she looked like someone with at least one child by now nearing puberty. She must live in the recurring worry of one day having to live with the choices her children would make.

"I'm going to put this in a frame, and hang it on my wall." I spoke finally, without waiting for her response which I bet would have been a controlled laughter. I picked up the sheet of paper and mumbled a hurried "Thank you", while resisting the strong urge to jump and scream.

But my curiosity was then immediately aroused, not as much for my own result as for the young man who had just gone before. By now he would already be out of the hospital, yet I wanted to run and catch up with him to ask all the questions in my head. But I delayed, wondering how easy it would be now to start up a conversation on the subject of his test without being at least a little improper. As I looked at the crimson sheet on which she had written the hyphenated words of the result, "non-reactive", I knew that I had been given a new blank slate without the strings of a thanksgiving church service that my mother would have recommended, had she known what I had just gone through. I had been reborn, no doubt. I threw the blood-stained blob of cotton in the nearby thrash bin, and then hopped again out of the charming Room Nine. I was just a few steps into the long corridors of the hospital ward when I found him, the young man. He was sobbing gently behind the door.

Behind the Door

Kola Tubosun is a student of language. Born in Ibadan, Nigeria, he studied Linguistics at the University of Ibadan, Moi University in Kenya, and Southern Illinois University, Edwardsville in the USA. He has published poetry in *Maple Tree Literary Supplement*, *AfricanWriter*, *Farafina*, *Sentinel Poetry Quarterly*, *Sentinel Nigeria*, *StoryTime*, *Subjective Substance*, *The Eintouist*, *Concelebratory Shoehorn Review* and poetry-in-translation in the *International Literary Quarterly*. His poem "Creation Story" won the 2002 Okigbo Poetry Prize in Nigeria. He also won the October 2006 Sentinel Poetry Bar Challenge with the poem titled *Here Moving*. He has worked as freelance journalist, translator, researcher, and a Fulbright foreign language teacher of Yoruba at Southern Illinois University, Edwardsville. Online Kola can be found on www.twitter.com/baroka and www.ktravula.com

African Roar

Yesterday's Dog

Masimba Musodza

It had been a long drive, and Stanley was beginning to doze off. Harare was less than 20 kilometres away on the Mutare Road. The radio was not working, and he had exhausted the four tracks that made up the only CD that he had in the Hyundai Tiburon. And the air-conditioning wasn't working, leaving him at the mercy of the October heat. He would have gladly stopped somewhere, but the need to get to Chitungwiza was urgent. Already, the sky to the west was tinged with mauve.

Stanley had shut his mind from the outside scenery. So, when the man appeared on the road, he seemed to have materialised from another dimension of his consciousness, an apparition from a half-remembered and uncomfortable dream. He recognised the man at once, and this is why he slammed on the brakes pedal. The tyres seemed to scream forever as the car slowed to a halt.

In the rear-view mirror, Stanley saw the man trot with a pathetic, hobbling gait, one arm flapping wildly. The man reached the side of the car and peered in. He produced a waft of body odour, sweat, tobacco and something else Stanley could not put his finger on.

"Are you going to Harare, Sir?"

That same voice! After so many years, it was the same voice!

"You're the Sir," Stanley countered, smiling affably, despite the fluttering in his stomach. "And, yes, I'm going to the big city. Jump in."

The man jumped in, slamming the door shut. His manner suggested that he was not accustomed to riding city cars, the demeanour of a man made conscious of his own social inferiority by the grandeur of his surroundings. Stanley marvelled at this; God, how much the man had changed! He wondered if he had made a mistake, if this perhaps was someone else.

As the man settled in, placing his stained, torn travel-bag on his lap, Stanley allowed himself a good look at his new passenger, saw the scar on his wrist that erased any lingering doubt about his identity. It was he, all right. That confirmation was the key that opened the door to a simmering hatred and a compelling desire to smash that wizened face into a pulp, rip those sinewy, thin limbs from that bony, pot-bellied torso. To wreak a terrible revenge on this former Rhodesian Security Forces man who had tortured him so long ago.

Stanley had been the brightest student in the Chiweshe area of central Mashonaland, the envy of many families, and the pride of his own. He had recently won a scholarship to study in the United Kingdom, and the village girls, always quick to recognise a man with a future beyond the local shopping centre, were throwing themselves at his feet. Even his brothers and cousins suddenly found their love lives immensely rewarding. Who would sneeze at the prospect of being at least the sister-in-law of the village's star?

This was the source of the problem; there wasn't enough of Stanley and his kinsmen to go around, even within the institution of polygamy. Supply could not meet demand.

And when Stanley quashed rumours of a match with the storekeeper Mhunga's daughter by marrying Netai, the daughter of the desperately poor widow Mufakose, the aggrieved storekeeper went to the police station and reported that Stanley was in with the *magandanga*, the nationalist guerrillas.

They came at the crack of dawn.

Stanley was in bed. Netai, his bride, was sweeping the yard. When the door to his hut creaked open, he thought she had come back, as she did sometimes, for one more moment of passion before everybody else woke up to place the hundred and one demands an extended family regards as the natural burden of the eldest son. But, instead, a giant Idi Amin of a man in combat fatigues stood in the doorway. Stanley snapped out of that state between asleep and awake with a start. Commotion could be heard behind the intruder; screams of protest and terror countered by rough accusations and threats.

"Stanley Chipatiso?" the soldier barked. It was more a confirmation than a desire for information. Another soldier appeared behind him. "Nyamhanza, don't waste time, man! Grab the terrorist bastard!"

Stanley felt rough hands grip and haul him out of bed as he had once hauled a rabbit out of a cage by its ears. Linen ripped, furniture smashed. He must have been resisting because he saw a huge, bony hand arc the air, and there was a loud slap. Stars danced before him and his face felt numb. Like that time, thinking the irascible old man was away visiting his son in the city, Stanley had allowed the cattle to wander into Nyati's maize field. That story had ended with a thorough beating.

He was being dragged across the just-swept yard, held face-up by the arms by two soldiers, while his heels ploughed the earth. The sun smashed into his eyes like a hammer. There was a sharp pain in his ribs. As if to answer the question forming in his mind, another soldier appeared and kicked him there.

Stanley howled like a wild animal with its paw in a trap.

"Shut up, *gandanga*!" someone snarled. Stanley could not see the speaker; the sun was in his eyes, a brilliant glare.

But he was sure this was the voice of a white man, the English had a heavy, guttural Dutch accent. "We are going to teach you a bladdy lesson, my boy!"

As he was hauled up on to the back of the truck, he saw Netai, writhing in the dust, screaming hysterically, her agony arising out of emotion rather than physical injury. These soldiers had come to get him, not beat up villagers. Well, not today.

His mother, emboldened by the apparent departure of the soldiers, emerged from a hut to console Netai. Other members of the family, all looking battered and tattered, were appearing. They watched him with the helplessness of livestock on the day of a feast as one of their own was taken away, with the same lack of knowledge of what was actually going to happen to him and the same apprehension.

Stanley contemplated the analogy, involuntarily shutting out the searing pain in his abdomen as the truck jiggled about over the rough dirt road. Was this why the Europeans called Native homesteads kraals, the same name given to cattle-pens? The people, his people, were like animals; they had lost their humanity to another people. A people whose right to so dehumanise them was that they had guns and a whole ideology apparatus, which said that they were right to do so because they were white and Stanley's people were not. They were to be herded, rounded up, confined to certain places and sustained only for whatever use they had been designated.

The truck had stopped. He was seized again, and he felt broken ribs dig in to his flesh. Then, his feet touched the ground.

"Let the bobjaan[1] walk by himself!" the white man ordered. Stanley turned to get a good look at him. He was too young to be in that uniform: slim, blond and crew cut, more like a Boy Scout. But here he was, in charge of all

---

[1] Afrikaans, "Baboon", racist slur.

these men, many of them old enough to be his father. And they were literally falling over each other to do his bidding.

There was also something about the blue chips of cold stone in his eyes that hinted at much more than a Boy Scout.

Stanley found himself feeling disappointed to see the white officer move in the opposite direction. Even though he knew that the problems Rhodesia was facing boiled down to the European Settlers' refusal to recognise the Natives as human beings, he believed that he could reason with them. After all, were not the Europeans going to send him to further his studies in their own land, something few Blacks could even dream of, attesting to his elevation to a higher status closer to them than to the rest of the Native Population? Why, he was one of those very few Natives the Europeans could, no should, trust. He could speak better English than these baboons who were at this moment kicking and punching him towards a windowless bungalow at the end of the police camp.

What was that word his headmaster had coined to designate those Africans who were yet to grasp even the rudiments of European civilisation, piscanemities?[2] Those who, having yet to adopt the use of toilet paper or any other trappings of civilisation, wiped their bottoms with sticks after a shit?

Please, Baas[3], you are my father! Stanley had seen his own father grovel and gush such obsequious drivel in gratitude to his master, Baas Koos de Vos, who had just given him three whole pairs of used underwear. Save me from the piscanemities, Baas!

But the little Baas had jumped into a jeep, shouting at one of his baboons to clamber in behind him.

---

[2] A crude play on *pisika*, the Shona word for the act of wiping after using the toilet, and Dog Latin.
[3] Afrikaans, "Boss", the correct way for a Black person to address a White male during colonial times.

"It's you educated ones that give us the problems!" one of the soldiers was saying. "You think we like to do this to you, we look on you as our little brother. But we have to, it's our job."

"Hopefully, when your mother sees what will be left of you, she's not going to let you cause trouble!" the other said, ominously. And so, like one of Dr Moreau's grotesque creations, Stanley was taken to the House of Pain. There, he felt the hand of he whose it was that wounded, and was chastised.

They broke three of his teeth, three of his ribs, a leg, and several fingers. They fried his genitals with electricity, and tested the water retention of his lungs by pouring the liquid down his throat with a teapot. In between, they took turns to beat him with sticks. It didn't matter that on the second day, Stanley confessed to his being a terrorist. On the third day, he begged them through a broken mouth to kill him.

Then, they took him to hospital. When his mother saw the ruins of his face, she fell to the floor, and uttered a soft moan, and had a stroke.

When he recovered from his torture, Stanley had run away to Mozambique to join the Comrades in the bush. He had never got the chance to fire a gun; the Lancaster talks happened and the Republic of Zimbabwe was born.

And now here he was, with one of the men who had tortured him sitting next to him in his own car. Stanley cast him a sidelong glance. How the mighty had fallen! Clearly, the wretch had only distant memories now to remind him that life could have meaning and purpose, memories of a life that ended when the last Rhodie had crossed the Limpopo to the last desperate bid to prop up the last bastion of the Master Race in South Africa. At least the Rhodies had, for a while, found something to justify all they believed they stood for. However, for this ex-*chimbwasungata*[4], there were only humiliating memories of

---

[4] Shona, "chained dog", what the nationalists called a Black collaborator.

discarded underwear, tins of beef. Scraps from the Master's table.

As that analogy entered his mind, Stanley reflected on the realisation that he was now the new dog, slobbering eagerly under the table of the new Master, and savagely mauling anyone who smelt wrong. Was he too to end up like this dried-up wasteland of a man? The man was talking in a provincial accent; about continued drought, the ever-increasing cost of living, the decimation of the population in his village by AIDS, the laziness of the youth, the failure of the Government to assist the starving villagers despite the fact that farms were now being given to Black people.

Stanley wasn't listening. He felt a tide of pure hatred rise in his heart. Hatred and desire for revenge.

How would he do it? The answer hit him immediately. Just around the bend was an out-of-the-way hotel. It was called a hotel only because the word "brothel" was not known to Zimbabwean Law. You were unlikely to get a room there, but you could get the girl that occupied that room.

It was not an entirely illegal set-up, inasmuch as the Law was in lacunae regarding much of the business that was transacted there. However, no one seemed to mind too much. After all, establishments like this hotel kept the swelling numbers of prostitutes and their clients off the streets and out of public view. That way, Zimbabwe maintained its self-righteous mantle, preserving its 'culture'.

Meanwhile, the hospitals were overcrowded, and the cemeteries sprawled.

Between the main road and the hotel lay a long stretch of bush. Any thing could happen in there, and no one who wasn't there need know about it. The bastard could squeal like a pig, and there'd be no one to hear him. Stanley could smash that gaunt, melancholic face to a pulp. Cut off those thin lips, transform that long face into a grinning death's head. He could simply break both his legs, which was as good as a death sentence to someone who lived in the rural areas.

Up ahead, the detour sign appeared. Stanley turned the car in. A look of surprise flitted across the other man's face. "I thought you were going into the city, my brother," he said, anxiously. His voice had a soft innocence to it, the voice of Abel as Cain led him in to that wilderness.

But this was different, Stanley told himself. This old man was no Abel, this was a monster. He had done things to him because he had the power then. That power, the power to hurt others, was now with Stanley.

"I just thought you might want to cool your throat," Stanley said, marvelling at the placidity of his own voice. "Get a taste of the city before we actually get there, you know!"

"You buying?" the man asked, eagerly.

"Of course!" Stanley grinned back. "Otherwise, I would not speak of such things to my big brother!"

The man chuckled. "Ah, verily you are Jesus of Nazareth!" he said. "If Fate appreciated that these are the waters that sustain us." He let the statement of sheer longing hang. "How our circumstances often deny us our deepest joys! Tonight, however, my brother, you have made me happy!"

Stanley resisted the urge to smash his fist into that thin, creased face. Bush, dark hulking shapes like the backdrop from the Blair Witch Project poster, rolled away on either side. All Stanley had to do was park and take this Rhodesian *chimbwasungata* for his last walk. Anyone passing would think nothing of a vehicle parked in the middle of the bush; many couples preferred the novelty of the bush to the claustrophobic seediness of the hotel.

Stanley pulled over. He looked at the man. "Best make room in the proverbial tank, eh? Thought I could hold till we go to the hotel, but my bladder's about to burst!"

He stepped out of the vehicle. What if the man did not follow? Of course he would. Leaving the vehicle for a leak was like how it was for women with their periods, when one started, it set off the others. What if he started the vehicle and drove off? Stanley dismissed the possibility. The Rhodesian Army had been highly mechanised, but it seemed unlikely they had ever taught their black troops anything above essential skills. And if he did drive off, well there was another reason to do him.

Stanley marched towards the bush. He heard the other man come up behind him. As he stopped beside him, and opened his fly, Stanley realised that he was not going to do it. He wasn't even going to beat him up. Killing him would not even the score. Nothing would.

He knew what he was going to do though.

He took him to the hotel bar and bought him a drink. The man grinned at the golden liquid topped by a thick layer of froth and clapped his hands loudly as Stanley set the glass flagon in front of him, and asked him his totem.

After he bought him his third drink, Stanley told him. As he wove that tapestry of torture, sometimes quoting verbatim, the man listened as King David must have the words of the Prophet Gad when he came to see him about Bathsheba. What little colour he had drained from him, and he began to tremble.

By the time Stanley had finished, the man was crying.

"My brother, how can I even begin to ask for forgiveness? We had to do it, it was the war! Please, look at me, I am a mere grave! Do you see a man who has been favourably rewarded for his deeds? My life has been hard, and when I sleep, those things that I did haunt me. I have been to all the churches, I have conducted appeasement sacrifices at the shrine of every tribe in this land, but there is no remission."

He bawled in between these lines, and the tears streamed. Some of the other patrons looked in their direction. "Please, my brother, if you want to kill me, go ahead. I am yours. But even you can see that there is nothing to kill here. Perhaps this is why the Ancestors let our paths cross again, so that you could see that the man you hate is no longer worthy even of death!"

"No, brother!" said Stanley, with conviction. "I no longer harbour a grudge." As he said those words, he realised them to be true. "It was war, and you did what you had to. Things change. Here we are now, drinking beer, in an independent Zimbabwe. What you did made me become a Freedom Fighter."

A couple more drinks later and they were on the road again. Stanley dropped him off in the city centre. He proceeded to Chitungwiza, to a place next to the Central Police Station.

A place surrounded by a concrete wall. As did most of the establishments in the area, except that this one did not have a placard or sign to tell people what it was for.

It did not need one. The only people who ever went there knew exactly the nature of the business they transacted at this complex. Those that were taken there soon found out. If they came back, they were never keen to tell outsiders. Speculation was rife, and the walls were associated with sinister goings-on.

For Stanley Chipatiso, Central Intelligence Organisation operative, the ability to regard the walled complex as simply the place where he worked had become something of a remarkable exercise in mental discipline. He specialised in interrogation, in getting ordinary folk apprehended for careless remarks on the bus or such like public place to confess that they were M.D.C activists in the pay of foreign, Western forces.

As he reported for work, he was given a list of people to talk to that evening. A printer whose employee, bitter at being demoted in favour of someone from a tribe he regarded as inherently inferior, had tipped the C.I.O that he was making posters for the M.D.C. Stanley knew that the allegation was false, but he too believed that tribe to be the scum of the earth and shared the rat's outrage. An old man who, after a few pints, had claimed to have worked as a chef at State House and had plenty to talk about the First Family.

Ah, further down the list was a writer who had posted articles on the internet. Stanley loved writers. He would read to them what they had written, and they would babble protests, denying ever having written that. He would explain to them that he hated doing it, but these writers left him with no choice.

The last one had begged Stanley to kill him, just as Stanley himself had so many years ago made a similar desperate plea to the old man he had bought drinks a few hours earlier. He was that old man now. What had been his name? Nyamhanza? It did not matter. He was Nyamhanza now. The name had faded from memory, and its owner would follow soon. But what he had stood for, hurt for, in the bigger scheme of things, lived on in Stanley.

He was walking down a corridor, silent and sterile as any in a hospital. He imagined that he heard the muffled sounds of an interrogation behind the doors he passed. It occurred to Stanley that one day, he too would be a broken, ragged man, bereft of the aegis of the system that sustained him now, commending himself to the mercy of those who were his victims.

He steeled himself against that poignant question, and turned the handle on the door to room 57.

African Roar

Born on the 29th of March 1976 in Harare, Zimbabwe, Masimba Musodza trained as a screenwriter. He burst on the literary scene with *The Man who turned into a Rastafarian*, an anthology of short-stories that has been listed as a definitive work of Rastafarian fiction. He has contributed to *StoryTime*, the most exciting fiction e-zine devoted to African writers. Musodza writes on a variety of subjects, but he is best known as the creator of *The Dread Eye Detective Agency* mystery/thriller stories.

The Nestbury Tree

Ayodele Morocco-Clarke

It all started to kick off when the Shepherd of the church located at the far side of the compound behind the house pronounced that the Nestbury tree in the yard was a haven for witches and had to come down.

Now, this was a church my parents had built and the Nestbury tree was a tree my grandfather had planted as soon as he bought the property. He had brought the Nestbury sapling from Kingston, Jamaica when he migrated to Lagos. It had been his most precious possession and he had guarded it diligently. That tree had been in the yard before my mother married my father. In fact, it was older than Mother herself and was a defining mark in our whole area of Igbobi in Lagos.

My grandfather was long dead before the Shepherd made his pronouncement about the Nestbury tree, and so was my father. Actually, neither of them had known the Shepherd before they died, which I think was extremely lucky for him as due to his erratic temper, Grandpa had had a ferocious reputation which preceded him all over the country. Rumours have it that some people surreptitiously referred to him as "the mad foreigner".

I really believe that if Grandpa had been alive, the Shepherd would not have dared utter those ridiculous words and if he had done so, he would probably have been dining with his ancestors in heaven or in hell not long after.

African Roar

That is how much my Grandpa loved his Nestbury tree. Daddy had told me years ago that Grandpa had had one of the gardeners whipped to within an inch of his life for daring to "trim" the branches of the tree without his authorisation and he had almost shot some thieving neighbourhood kids who had sneaked in to steal fruit from the tree. Nobody messed with the Nestbury tree and everyone in the community knew this unwritten rule.

Grandpa had obviously instilled his great love for his Nestbury tree in my mother because she guarded it almost as jealously as he had. She swore that it was the only tree of its kind in the whole country and to this very day I believe her because in all my sojourns throughout Nigeria, I have never seen another tree like it.

Mum took great pride in the Nestbury tree as one would a unique and gifted child. I often wondered how she would have felt towards the tree had she been the one who brought it all the way from Jamaica.

The pronouncement made by the Shepherd, followed by the death sentence he passed on the tree, seemed to unleash a demon in Mum when she learned of it. She stormed over to the church and started yelling that it was only going to be over her dead body that anyone would cut down the Nestbury tree. The Shepherd just looked on unperturbed and told her that whether she liked it or not the tree was going to come down. He reiterated his opinion that the tree was used by witches as a meeting place and that this could clearly be seen by anyone as there were always bats hovering around and nesting in the tree.

"You are a good-for-nothing illiterate who knows nothing about plants or animals," Mum shouted. "I want this church out of my compound as soon as possible. When my husband and I built this church many years ago, we did not intend to be stabbed in the back by a conniving bunch of idle traitors."

"You are a witch," taunted the Shepherd. "That's why you don't want us to cut the tree down. You and your coven meet there every night and now that we know your secret, you want to hide under the umbrella of plants and animals."

I stared aghast at the Shepherd. In all my life, I had never heard anyone speak so rudely or disdainfully to her. Mum looked like she was going to explode. But remarkably, she sucked in her breath and calmly told the Shepherd that she would be getting in touch with the church headquarters to have him removed from her property.

"I have seen off bigger and better men than you. You are definitely no match for me," she concluded and turned on her heels, gesturing at me to follow.

"Afefe ti fe furo adie ti wa nita," (the wind has blown and we can see the fowl's bottom), the Shepherd continued to taunt at her retreating back in Yoruba. I felt like slapping his stupid smirking face.

Thus began the battle between my mother in one corner and the church, led by the Shepherd, in the other.

The day after the confrontation between my mother and the Shepherd, seven members from the church came to the house. They were known as the Church Elders Committee and were led by the Elder Ojo who was the chairman. I went to open the front door when they rang the bell and Elder Ojo asked to see Mum. I made them wait outside while I went to ask her if she wanted to see them. Experience had taught me not to let anyone in without obtaining approval from my mother. Mum was not happy to hear that the church elders had come to see her. She was still sour from her encounter with the Shepherd, but told me to let them in.

I returned to the front door and ushered them all into the receiving hall. Mum made them wait about ten minutes before she went to meet them.

"Ekaale, Ma," chorused the elders in Yoruba; my ear was planted firmly to the door leading to the hall.

"Good Evening."

Speaking up, the Chairman addressed Mum in Yoruba. Apparently he had stood up because I heard Mum ask him to sit down.

"We are here because we were informed of the altercation that occurred between you and the Shepherd yesterday evening."

"What about it?" Mum's voice was raised and I heard one of the coffee tables clatter to the floor.

"We think that it is bad that things got out of hand yesterday and we are convinced that the disagreement only happened because there was no elder on hand to bring the situation under control," the Chairman continued. "The Shepherd had no right to call you a witch and he has been admonished."

"That is not good enough." An even higher octave. "I want him off my property, and if you people do not agree, you can all go with him. I have telephoned the Pastor at the church headquarters, and he is sending a representative here before the end of the week."

"But Ma, you shouldn't have taken such drastic action before informing the Committee," the Chairman protested, to which I heard murmurs of approval.

"It's my church, and I can do whatever I please," Mum snapped in English. "I'll be damned if I'm going to sit around idle while some nonentity nitwit calls me a witch. What has my Nestbury tree done to him that he wants to destroy it?"

"But Ma," another voice said. I was not sure who it was, though I thought the voice belonged to Elder Abiodun, a man who did not like Mum one little bit. "That tree is not a good tree. It is evil, and at night you can see strange birds flying around it. They don't go to any other tree, only that one. Moreover, strange noises always come from the tree at night."

"Bats," said Mum. "Bats live in that tree, that is why you hear noise around the tree, and they are the so-called "strange birds" you say fly around the tree. Anyway, I don't care what any of you say. That tree is staying, and if you people don't like it you can all go to hell."

I heard a collective gasp from the elders. I scrambled to my feet and quickly moved away from the door because I knew that with that blasphemous pronouncement, the meeting would end soon, and I did not want to be caught eavesdropping.

A few minutes later, the door to the hall opened and the elders filed out. I opened the front door and bade them goodnight with a smirk on my face, knowing that my mother was not going to be cowed on the matter.

Two days after the elders came to the house, the Pastor's representative came to see my mum. He said he decided to come to the house before proceeding to the church, as the pastor had told him to hold peace talks with my mother and the Shepherd. He said he had also been told to deliver a sermon on unity, and that was why he had not come earlier, as he wanted to deliver the sermon at the Sunday service when there would be a full congregation to hear the message.

Mum was unhappy with this news. She was incensed. When she had spoken to the pastor, she had made it clear that she wanted the Shepherd off her property, and that she was not interested in any conciliatory talks. She wasted no time in telling the Pastor's representative this. He was quick to placate her, quoting passages from the Scripture and telling her that as the matron of the church, she was supposed to be slow to anger and quick to forgive.

His words must have touched a chord deep inside her, because after some further persuasion, Mum allowed herself to be cajoled into attending the church service that morning. This was an achievement on the part of the pastor's representative, as Mum had previously sworn that she would not set foot inside the church until that upstart of a Shepherd was gone.

I was not going to miss out on the action, so I went to put on my church gear whilst Mum got ready for church. In no time, we set off for the church through the back door of the house with the Pastor's representative in tow. The church was fenced off from the compound to give us some privacy. However, we had a private entrance from the compound leading directly to the front of the church which Mum had kept locked since the day she fell out with the Shepherd. She did not want anyone sneaking into the compound to cut down the Nestbury tree.

The service had already begun when we got to the church, and a hush fell over the congregation as we entered. I could see some people craning their necks to see who was with Mum, and others beginning to whisper amongst themselves. Having heard about the altercation between Mum and the Shepherd, they looked like they were hoping for a showdown.

Mum proceeded to her special matron's seat while the representative of the pastor went up to take a seat at the church altar. I blended in with the people who were sitting towards the back. From my seat, I could see Elder Abiodun frowning and fidgeting in his seat. Nobody knew that the pastor's representative was on a peace mission, and people continued to whisper to one another. I even overheard two women predicting that the Shepherd was not going to last the night at the parish.

Upon seeing the Pastor's representative, the Shepherd looked nervous and quite agitated. At that moment, I cursed the pastor for advocating peace and unity. He should have done away with the Shepherd instead of playing the peacemaker.

The service proceeded as normal with hymns and prayers. After the second reading of the Bible, it was time for the sermon, and the Pastor's representative gestured to the

Shepherd that the sermon was going to be delivered by him and not the person originally scheduled to do so.

Stepping up to the pulpit, he proceeded to talk about Christianity and the concept of brotherhood. "It is not uncommon for people have clashes with other people, what matters is that at the end of it, they come out stronger and united. We all have to learn to be tolerant of one another as we are one in Christ. We must be our brother's keeper, slow to anger and quick to forgive. If someone offends you, call him and tell him where he has gone wrong. Please do not bear a grudge. Love your neighbour as you do yourself."

Asking the congregation to get to its feet, the Pastor's representative proceeded to sing a hymn in the middle of the sermon:

Let there be love shared among us,
Let there be love in our heart.
May now your love sweep this nation,
Cause us O Lord to arise.
Give us a fresh understanding,
Of brotherly love that is real.
Let there be love shared among us,
Let there be love.

He concluded by saying that God was the creator of all things, and if the Lord was not happy with anything, he will in his divine wisdom take care of that thing. He said that if anyone felt that they were being oppressed by evil forces, they should take it to the Lord in prayer, and they would be surprised that God does actually answer prayers.

Unfortunately, the pastor's representative did not know that he had unwittingly sowed a seed that was to germinate in the Shepherd's mind. His words were to form the basis for the Shepherd to launch a stinging attack on the Nestbury tree, and by extension, my mother.

African Roar

A couple of days after the representative's sermon, word came to Mum that the Shepherd had told the congregation that there was to be a night vigil which was to run for seven days at the church premises starting on Friday night. The aim of the vigil was to bring the Nestbury tree down. The vigil was to be done "Jericho style"; the people would gather and march round the Nestbury tree singing, chanting and praying that the tree would fall down the way the walls of Jericho had in the Bible after the Israelites laid siege on the city of Jericho.

Mum was not pleased about this latest development. It annoyed her to no end that the Shepherd had acted like a hypocrite and pretended that the issue with the tree was well and truly over. I on the other hand thought that the Shepherd had finally lost the plot. He seemed so obsessed with the tree that he had lost all sense of reasoning. I immediately saw a massive flaw with the Shepherd's vigil plan because Mum had taken to locking the private entrance leading from the compound to the church, and there was no means for the congregation to actually march round the Nestbury tree since they did not have access to it anymore.

However, the minor issue of lack of access to the tree was not going to deter the Shepherd. He decided that they would hold a modified version of the Jericho style vigil. According to his revised plan, the congregation would gather by the church fence at the spot nearest to the tree. Once there, they were to point their fingers, and direct their prayers and chants at the tree. This was to be done daily from 12 midnight till 6 a.m. for seven days. He informed them that if they kept vigil diligently and performed their prayers with faith and conviction, the evil tree would fall down like the walls of Jericho did.

I was amused when I heard this, but Mum was not. She looked more than a little perturbed. I thought that the Shepherd had finally taken leave of his senses and I was determined to avoid a situation where he or his cohorts would sneak into the compound while everyone was asleep at night to cut down the tree. I informed Adamu, the security guard to keep a vigilant eye on the Nestbury tree and the entire area leading to the church. He was under Mum's strict instructions to shoot any intruders he found in the leg.

On Friday night, we were in the house when we heard the vigil begin at midnight. I could not help laughing as I thought that there were many gullible people who were depriving themselves of much needed sleep in pursuit of an elusive goal. Like real sheep, they were being led by the Shepherd of the church without stopping to question the path he was leading them along.

The vigil continued for seven days. The pattern was the same; chanting, singing and praying. For every one of those seven days, I woke up early in the morning and went to check that nothing had happened to the tree. Mum did the same. By the sixth day, I was already smug with thoughts of victory thinking of ways in which I would ridicule the deluded Shepherd. I kept wondering why the church members were bothering to waste their time coming for the vigil when it was apparent that nothing could happen to the tree. I could not for the life of me fathom how the Shepherd hoped to accomplish his goal on this last day in light of the fact that all his past efforts had proved abortive.

On Thursday night, I sat with Mum in the living room and watched the news like we did every night. It had been a beautiful day and the weatherman said the good weather was going to continue over the weekend with less than five percent risk of precipitation. Earlier in the day, word had come to Mum that at the mid-week service the night before, the Shepherd had told the congregation that the vigil on Thursday night was to start at 9 p.m. and carry on through out the night until daybreak. I felt this was his last desperate bid to secure the downfall of the Nestbury tree. Predicting his failure, I wondered what he would say to the tired idiots who had shunned their cosy beds in favour of waging a war against a tree.

I went to bed against the now familiar backdrop of chanting, singing and praying which had become the norm over the last six days. On this night however, the chants and prayers were louder and sounded much more ferocious. I snuggled up in bed and eventually fell asleep.

I jerked awake to solid blackness. There had been a power cut. The wind was howling outside and there was a storm raging. I could hear things being flung about outside and some doors or windows that had no locks slamming shut repeatedly. At intermittent periods, I saw flashes of lightning followed closely by terrible bursts of deafening thunder.

I peeked out of my window and could make out the shapes of the dogs huddled together on the piazza. Whenever there was a streak of lightening, I could see them clearly for a split second. A few of them were howling piteously.

Not for the first time, I cursed the incompetent Nigerian Meteorological Service. It was less than five hours since the dumb weatherman had said the weather was going to be beautiful. This was almost as bad as the hurricane blunder Michael Fish made in England all those years ago.

Settling back into bed, I tried to fall asleep. My ears, however, picked up a strange noise. It was not the rain and though it sounded like a rumble, it was not thunder. Incredulously, I realised what the sound was. It was the chanting of the church members. They were roaring with prayers. I could faintly hear the clapping of many hands as well as what seemed to be the stamping of a great number of feet, and I could not believe that anyone would be out in this appalling weather.

I came to the swift conclusion that religion could be a powerful weapon when wielded in the hands of the misguided and even more so when used to lead the ignorant. This was fanaticism at its worst. I fell into a deep but troubled sleep, only to be woken less than an hour later. Once again, I woke up startled. This time, however, what made me wake up was a mighty crash, which caused my bed to vibrate. I could feel the earth shake beneath me, making me wonder if the house was collapsing. I dashed out of my room and almost collided with Mum in the corridor. The loud crash had woken her as well. As there was still no power supply, we lit some candles and walked from one room to another, ensuring that everything was in order and that nothing was damaged.

Neither Mum nor I could go back to sleep after that. We stayed awake and sat in the lounge speculating about what might have caused the loud bang and made the earth to vibrate so violently. I came up with some earthquake theories, citing ground movements in California and Mexico to buttress my point. I kept telling Mum that we needed to flee the house because it might disappear into some crevice soon and she kept retorting "Don't be silly" or "Don't be daft," saying we were safer indoors than we would be outside in the storm. After a while, I gave up and shut up. I could see that Mum was worried and more than once, I wondered if I should be worried too.

The storm abated about forty-five minutes later and not long afterwards, we could see the nimble but tentative fingers of dawn stealthily snaking across the sky. The dogs had long stopped howling and everywhere seemed eerily quiet, like a deserted battlefield. The silence was broken by a cock crowing, followed by another, then another.

Mum told me to go and get the two hurricane kerosene lanterns we kept in the pantry. When I brought them to her, she lit both of them, passed one back to me and ordered me to follow her. We were going on an inspection tour of the whole compound to determine the extent of damage the storm might have wrought.

We exited from the front entrance of the house and made our way towards the western-most part of the compound with the lanterns boosting the visibility that was available from the poor natural light of the daybreak. The compound looked like a mini-war zone. There was chaos everywhere, with debris strewn wherever our eyes touched. Many of the trees had been stripped of most of their fruit and leaves, and there were mangoes, paw paws, almonds, oranges, avocado pears and a few coconuts lying on the ground in disarray. The banana and plantain plants had collapsed under the barrage of the wind and heavy rain with their fruits lying limply on the ground. The corrugated roofing sheets which had been stacked neatly next to the security-guard's outpost were all over the place, grotesquely bent and twisted out of shape. My eyes took in the scene of disarray, before coming to settle on a gap in the fence next to the front gate where the wall had collapsed.

By this time, the dogs had run up to us, their tails wagging gleefully. I did not share their morning enthusiasm and tried to shoo them away from the fence, to prevent them from running out of the compound. Mum had been strangely quiet all this while and I wondered what could have been running through her head. Together, we gathered a few of the roofing sheets strewn about and tried to make a temporary barrier to cover the gap in the fence. We secured them with some of the large mortars and blocks from the collapsed fence.

When we were through, it was already light and Mum said that we needed to take a look at the rest of the compound. Cutting round the utilities wing of the house, Mum abruptly came to a halt, causing me to run into her back. I heard her sharp intake of breath and tried to peer past her to see what had made her stop so suddenly. The sight that greeted my eyes was unbelievable. Where I had thought there had been chaos up front, mayhem greeted us at the back of the compound. But all these paled into insignificance at the sight of the Nestbury tree lying full length on the ground, completely uprooted, with the topmost point of the tree less than two feet from the house. If the tree had been a human being, I would have said that it lay spread-eagled on the ground. Paradoxically, it looked quite resplendent in the midst of the debris, as if it had decided to take a little nap after standing in all its glory for so many years.

Fascinated, I moved over closer to the Nestbury tree and tried to inspect the exposed roots. It had been uprooted like a seedling in a nursery. I had never seen anything like it in all my fifteen years on earth. Realisation dawned on me that this must have been responsible for what I had earlier speculated to be an earthquake.

There was a strange moaning emanating from Mum as she knelt beside the crown of the fallen tree. She looked as if she had been pole-axed. Never had I allowed myself to entertain the thought that the Nestbury tree would end up like this.

Mother wept.

I had never seen Mum cry like she did that morning. Big, wracking sobs that shook her body. The tears ran down her cheeks in torrents and looked for a while like the Nigerian map showing the Niger and Benue rivers running separately before merging in a confluence on her chin and finally dribbling off to the ground.

Mum's tears seemed bizarre to me, as I had always known her to be tough, strong and a pillar to be relied on when a person was in distress. Now she was apparently in distress herself. She cried like she had lost one of her children.

I became absorbed with trying to work out how the Shepherd had accomplished the impossible, and I was surprised when I felt Mum's hand grasping my elbow. Her eyes were red and swollen, making her look like she had developed a sudden attack of conjunctivitis. When she suggested that we proceed indoors, her voice sounded hoarse; rasping. In less than one hour, she seemed to have aged several years. Oddly, she stooped as she walked, leaning heavily on my arm and causing me on more than one occasion to stagger.

Once inside the house, Mum went to her room and immediately took to her bed. This was very unusual, as she could never be caught in bed once the sun was up. She gave me strict instructions that she did not want to be disturbed by anyone. Under no circumstances was I to let any visitor into the house.

Mum stayed in bed all day, refusing to come out of her room despite my pleas. All efforts to cajole her to eat some food failed. At intermittent intervals, I heard mutterings and sobbing coming from her room.

By nightfall, I felt helpless and made a resolve to go early the next morning to see Mum's brother, Uncle Jacob, to intimate him of the day's event.

Very early the next morning, I went to Mum's room to find out if she was feeling better. I knocked a few times, but did not hear her call out to me to enter. Afraid that she might snap at me if I woke her up, I retreated to my room to get ready to go to Uncle Jacob's house.

I took a shower and after dressing up, I went back to Mum's room to inform her that I was going out. Again, I knocked on her door and still she did not answer, so I eased the door open.

She was lying in bed asleep.

"Mum, I'm going to Uncle Jacob's," I said.

There was no reply. I thought this was strange, as she was such a light sleeper.

"Mum," I called.

"Mum?" I went to open the drapes. Yet she slept on.

With the first few rays of the early morning sun now streaming into the bedroom, I turned to my mother on the bed. There was a knot of anxiety growing at the bottom of my belly as I tentatively reached out my hand to shake her gently.

"Mum, Mum," I called again very softly, almost whispering.

Still she remained motionless.

The Nestbury Tree

"Mum?" By now, I was shaking her vigorously, my voice trembling as I called her with urgency, trying to quell the rising hysteria that threatened to overwhelm me.

"Mum, MUM, Mummmmmmmmmm," I screamed, clawing at her desperately, tears streaming down my face.

I could hear a high-pitched ululating noise escaping from somewhere in the house and did not realise that it came from me. I continued screaming even after strong arms pried me away from my mother's dead body.

Ayodele Morocco-Clarke is a writer of mixed heritage and an award winning Solicitor and Advocate of the Supreme Court of Nigeria. Describing herself as stubbornly unconventional, she is the editor of *Critical Literature Review* and her written works have appeared in *Author Africa 2009, Saraba Magazine, Hackwriters* (a University of Portsmouth magazine), *Sphere Literary Magazine, StoryTime* and on *The Clarity of Night* blog. Ayodele hopes to publish an anthology of short fiction soon and is currently working on her first novel.

African Roar

Cost of Courage

Beaven Tapureta

I kept walking on the dark, deserted road. I was with it again, like an incurable mental illness which came with ghastly voices and visions. My eyes hardly blinked; demons played wild soccer in the natural turf of my mind, howling, "Punch him down! Punch him down!" I whispered to myself that I was not going to fall or be punched down by whatever or whoever those demons were. The darkness, like social exclusion's tinted eyes, looked at me from a precarious viewpoint. Then the wild soccer suddenly ceased, was replaced with ear-splitting shouts not such as one hears from a football stadium: "Cry Freedom! Cry Freedom! Cry Freedom!" I had watched the film *Cry Freedom* and it stung me with memories of Black Consciousness. The throaty screams became harsher and harsher like war cries grinding against buttocks of guns, drowning in teargas and blood: "Cry Freedom...! Cry Freedom! FREEEEEEERRRRDOOOOOMMMMMMMM CRRRRRRYYYYY!"

The crumbling, blasting and splitting of gun-sound, the voices and the sharp squeal of stampeding women and children combined into a festival of ghosts. I ran blindly like a fugitive. Unexpectedly, I found a bloodied spoor which led me to the mountains in a certain black kingdom on whose gates was the name Zimbabwe, written in sweat and blood. The kingdom's gates were locked to the hilt.

"Is anyone home?" I screamed. "FATHER! FATHER! I am home!" But father was nowhere to be found...

Suddenly, my eyes opened. My clothes were damp as I beat away the blankets. The dream disappeared as fast as it had come. And even in reality, father was nowhere to be found; only the blankets, sweat, and the distant decibels of an already busy morning. The sun peeped through the doorway like a bearer of empty news.

My friend named Brother, a poetry freak, carried a fire-child inside of him only sated by pen and paper. I confess I knew very little about him, he talked less and wrote more. Brother's poetry was the resilient music of a bird flying over the burning bushes, chirping on top of its individual pain and struggle.

Despite my terrible dream, that afternoon I visited Brother to wish him a happy thirtieth birthday.

"I am getting old and I have no proper job, see," he said, his voice a bit watered down by self-pity. His sullen lips twitched as if he was under a great desire to talk but the words were just being pulled back into his belly.

"I have dreams, Kenny", he said after a while.

I wanted to tell him about my dream but dismissed the thought. Instead, I said, "And one day the dreams shall come true," yet still I felt my voice was an insufficient salve upon his wretchedness. I fixed my eyes on the empty pots and plates scattered on the floor. Brother said nothing, locked his lips in silence again.

Brother's room had a writing corner occupied by an old desk and chair weighed down by books and manuscripts lying one over another like mating frogs. From a file on the desk he pulled out a photocopied poem and handed it over to me.

"Recently published in an international magazine called Voices and Verses," he said.

"A brilliant birthday present for you from Mother Muse". I smiled.

Cost of Courage

He looked at me and said, "I feel identified by the world. I am a bream swimming from the gloomy waters towards the shores of glory, yet there are storms and hungry sharks following. Very sad indeed."

"Break out of that vicious circle of negativity, Brother," I said, passing his poem back to him. He nodded, and looked away.

Afterwards, we talked about other issues before I left him and went back to my one-roomed house a short distance away.

I watched, during the sizzling days, school-less children running around the shabby ghetto houses which blind-walled and nurtured them into thugs, murderers, rapists; hungry mothers walking to the shops where there was nothing to purchase, fathers sweating as they tussled with wage-less work in the industries. The ghetto was nothing but a community of empty clothes, littered dust streets, slapdash houses overstuffed with misery, and lots of toilets which got more visits from cholera victims. Hunger and indigestion, the people's daily meal.

Yet we carried a peculiar beauty we did not know about, a beauty which existed underneath the hunger-tortured pigskin of our faces, a light beneath the un-shed tears in our eyes and wisdom in our soft words. I did not want to pity too much because I knew inside us, and in our silence, was a strength which only time would tell.

One day I boarded an overloaded bus to the city centre. The music in the bus drowned the loud passengers' voices. As the bus moved, I realised that the windows were closed. I stood in the crowded aisle. We stood so close to each other that there was no space for breathing. Soon I began to feel vertigo, and before I knew it, my feet melted and darkness covered my eyes.

Later, I found myself perspiring and sitting on the seat where a certain young lady had been. Two men had removed my shirt and shoes and were urging other passengers to give me some more space. The conductor looked very worried. The driver had slowed down the bus.

"How are you feeling now?" the lady who gave up the seat was the first to ask me.

I looked around. All eyes were pinned on me.

My head was heavy like a ball of steel. What had happened to me?

Three young men at the back seat stifled their laughter when one of them, assuming I was starving, whispered, "*Inzara iyo.*"

When I got off the bus in town I could not understand why I had fallen. As I crossed the street, I remembered the moon-face of an angel who had given up her seat for me. She had gone with a piece of me and I wished I could see her again and thank her. And yet, some encounters never repeat themselves.

After roaming around the industries near the city looking for a job, I came to the OK supermarket where lots of people who wanted to purchase bread stood in a long queue. I was thinking of joining the queue, yet I also wanted to go home. My money was not enough.

The sun gave in to the dark umbra covering the sky.

The heart of the city brimmed with people. I was in a bus queue, and behind me stood a young woman who was approached by a man in dark, baggy jeans, an over-sized "50 CENT" T-shirt and tan Caterpillar shoes with chains for laces; in his right hand a Samsung D780 Dual SIM glittered like a magic box. As he talked to her his hands waved up and down until he pointed to a Peugeot parked across the road. She smiled. They walked across the road to the Peugeot. The car sped away soon after she jumped in.

On my way back home, I first went to Brother's house and found him sitting quietly in his "writing corner". He regarded me with sad eyes that told me he wanted to say something.

Cost of Courage

"As I tell it to you now I am seeing it like a vision. The kombi kindly drops my father at the shopping center and he hurries home, patting a copy of *The Herald* against his thigh as he moves like a hero. My sister Nomalanga, six years old, and I, thirteen years old then, are in the dining room. Something is going on. There's a delicious smell in the kitchen where mother has been baking some cookies for the next day's lunch at school. Now she is in the bedroom, doing some work known only to her.

When father comes into the house he can tell things are not okay between Nomalanga who is sprawled on the floor fiddling with a ball pen in her hand and me, sadly staring at the writing pad on the sofa. I have some homework I want to do but naughty Nomalanga makes sure she has my pen to herself and mom has failed to settle things between us. We have been fighting over the pen and as usual I have given up. Nomalanga jumps in joy when she sees father walking into the house.

"Dad, dad," she calls.

"Hey little darling," father says, opening his arms and she jumps in. He dangles and carries her to the sofa. As he sits down, he looks at me. I look back at him with un-blinking and defiant eyes.

"Hi, sonny," father says but I remain downcast. Father then authoritatively says, "I said hi, what's the matter?"

Father's voice frightens and encourages me at the same time so I open my mouth and report, "She took my pen. I have homework. My teacher will beat me up tomorrow if I don't do my homework."

Nomalanga indifferently scribbles something on her palm. She says to father, "Look, dad, I write very well than him." She shows father what she has drawn on her palm. "A bird," she says. Father laughs but he knows how to play it the diplomatic way when dealing with Nomalanga.

"Can I borrow your pen for a moment?" father says to Nomalanga who winces back and doesn't want to give away the pen but then knowing that father is a strict man, she reluctantly hands over the pen to him. As father makes a gesture to pass the pen over to me she screams like a mad cricket and furiously retrieves the pen from father's hand.

We were like this, with our little squabbles…"

Brother became silent. I wanted to laugh but I could see he was so attached to his story, so I let him go on.

"So father gives her back the pen and pats me on the back as he stands up and whispers to me, "Don't worry." He goes to the bedroom singing, "Pam-pa-pa-p-ava-v-a Pam… Should-I-say-yes, should-I-say-no?" Nomalanga follows him to the bedroom, shouting behind him. "Dad, dad, give me paper to write on." She has torn out pages and used up all my note books; father just grabs a blank paper from somewhere in the bedroom's book-rack and gives it to Nomalanga.

Mother's unworried by all the sounds blowing in the house.

I am sitting on the sofa, resigned, but still clutching my books and writing pad, without a pen. It was on this very evening that I began to view the pen as an important tool in my life. I now see myself crying for a certain pen in this world. It was unfortunate that the next day father died in a car accident. Father's death caused total disintegration. The home and property were seized by family relatives and Nomalanga went to live with Uncle at the MacDonald Farm miles away. I grew up here in the ghetto where my mother was dumped by her in-laws and I don't know where she is. For me now life is a fiendish rogue that haunts the tired terrains of my memories."

On and on Brother talked, and by the time his voice died out, I was hungry. It was dark when I left Brother's place. As I walked home, the ghetto boomed around me with an exhibitionistic night in which sordid things happened. Girls and men slithered in and out of shanty brothels and drove away in sporty cars from which thundered out mutinous, obtrusive lyrics. Underneath this liveliness barked rhythms of fatal desire. From somewhere, one or two houses away, I heard screams likely to have been from a girl muffled under the heavy weight of a father-businessman-politician-church-leader-AIDS-sucking-fucker! On to my left there was this incomplete building, part of a clinic project onto which the MP only added a brick when election time comes. I didn't want to think about the MP, I wanted to go home and think about Brother's story.

Back in my room I gazed at a picture on the wall of my mind, of workers putting up an extension to the existing house of hunger. I felt poor, betrayed and I knew Brother was probably feeling the same where he was. My thoughts skirted around the present situation and I began to see everything in policy formats. My being unemployed was somebody's policy. The type of my life was also somebody's policy. My clothes, their shabbiness, the hunger in the ghetto, Brother's daily worries, the deadly night life in the ghetto, the untreated water we drank from the rusty taps and the cholera.

Still, the undying voices of people outside my house brought to my ears details of an un-stoppable quest for fulfilment. Life just hung everywhere like a nameless fruit over-ripening towards a nameless decomposition. My candle burnt like a flood-light that swallowed all shadows of tomorrow.

Brother visited me the next morning at exactly nine. He squinted at me, from top to bottom before he sat on the only chair I owned. "I have been to the shops. The prices of cooking oil, sugar, mealy meal, all things have gone up, for the fifth big time in a month," he said.

I looked down at the floor to avoid his penetrative stare. I did not open my mouth. He went on.

"I have an idea. What about border jumping into Botswana or Joza?"

"What for, Brother?" I asked.

"Survival," he said.

"Are you out of your mind?"

"Nope!"

"This is ridiculous. If you get caught you…"

Brother rose to his feet suddenly. "If I don't see you tomorrow take good care of yourself," he said.

I thought he was joking but he made it to the door.

"You are not serious Brother. Why don't you sit down and let us talk about some other alternatives, eh?"

"I will find alternatives beyond the Limpopo." Then he left.

I closed the door and buried myself under a blanket. The idea of a morning ceased to exist. A dark cloud slowly hung over my eyes and it was after half an hour of wafting in deep thought that sleep snatched me and a beautiful stretch of land began to unfold slowly. Happy families and well-fed girls and boys skittered and jumped in joy; harmony ruled everywhere, people socialised without worries about groping for a living in empty darkness. I liked this world, the opposite of what I had dreamt of before. I liked the beautiful children who came to me and begged me, "Kenny can you make kites for us! Make kites for us!" I liked the joy of playing with the kids free from the shooting guns of hunger, disease and abuse. The men and women in this land did not know of any injustice, of any segregation, social, political, economic. Instead they sweated together, enjoyed together, cried together, and struggled together to build one country. They spoke one language of survival. Their government was the government of the whole people. The person whom they respected and feared was one. Only God. And only God. Nobody else, nothing else, transcended this truth. No man, no animal, was supposed to take their freedom and gormandise it for self-fattening goals. If there was commotion, the women and men formed a shield that blocked the enemy's spears from piercing their children.

I liked to play with the kids on the lawns. A short big boy (SBB) came running at me and he hit me in the face. I fell to the ground heavily and yelled as if in pain, "Wow, wow,

wow." Then I feigned crying. SBB came over to me and knelt beside me; he reached out his hand and pulled me up, begging me to stop crying. I told him I was not crying but he said I should stop crying so that he can also not cry. Tears were a symbol of someone in pain. Only love could quell pain. The children did not like pain although they would pretend to feel it when I softly beat their little heads. They felt love. And they loved; SBB was transferring such love to me. I grabbed him into the crook of my hands and laughed to show him I was happy with him, that I was not crying. I liked this world... this beautiful, innocent world. And I knew Brother would like it too if he were here with me. Yet this world, beautiful world, was not there when I woke up in the afternoon.

When I met Brother the next day he told me of a different dream he had had. I was happy he hadn't crossed the Limpopo.

"I was in the middle of a hailstorm when a man called me from afar. I walked over to him and the man stretched his hand to greet me. This is what the man said to me: 'You are looking for me daily yet I am with you, within you. I am you. You grope but can't find me. So much dirt you absorb from outside yourself while inside you there is so much beauty if only you had eyes to look without fear. I am not God. I'm you.' Suddenly, I realised he was my double, he was me and he vanished.

The scene changed suddenly and I was in this place of nobility, being crowned king, and just when I was standing up to wave my hands in joy to the crowd, I woke up. So I am totally flummoxed," Brother said as he looked at me, deeply worried. He, as usual, abruptly stood up and left.

I did not see him for some days after we shared our dreams. I visited his home but he was nowhere to be seen. His neighbour told me Brother seemed to have found a house or a job somewhere else because he no longer came back home.

African Roar

Days and months snip off the calendar and still Brother does not appear. It is like I am waiting for him to come back and tell me stories about his adventures. This morning it's cold and windy in the city. I am walking along First Street, my mind fogged up with conflicting thoughts about where to find work. I am thinking Brother has probably found work in the industries. Maybe he's in jail. Maybe he has crossed the Limpopo after all. I have looked for him all over the ghetto, day and night, but have not located him. Neighbours don't even have a clue about his whereabouts. I can't forget about Brother, the stories he told me about his mother, sister, father, just can't! One day somewhere in the city I will find him. I could hear him talk in the silence of my mind. "I will find alternatives beyond the Limpopo."

The city is like a home of widowed and orphaned ghosts. Faces bypassing me on the street are smeared with an insipidness too wearisome to look at; they look at me like they want to dig out the very last small piece left of me now. I watch the grey spectacle around me concluding itself into a showbiz of hunger. Elderly beggars have awoken from their beds of flattened cardboard boxes in the nooks of the disused stinking city buildings. Street children snatch food from the unsuspecting ladies cat-walking in and out of the expensive food outlets, fashion shops and hair salons, blind beggars sing religious songs on the pavements to attract alms, their voices add music to the already discontent aura in the city as their silver plates ring loudly with each coin tossed by the passers-by.

I walk, my head rocking this and that way, and sometimes talking to myself, looking ahead as if my eyes are casting out for a better sight. I reach the foot bridge across Julius Nyerere Avenue and wait there like I am waiting for someone.

I leave the foot bridge a few minutes later and walk past the bakeries and fashion shops exuding this slow sad music. It's like the scent of a fresh delicious promise of an extended marriage with hunger, slow sad music which suddenly reminds me of Brother whose poems I read almost every day... bread and butter issues. I miss him so much, an artist lonely at heart.

I cross the street, my eyes look at the woman dressed in opulent clothes that expose some parts of her body, and she looks at me as if she were rereading a letter she read many years ago, a letter from a Farm-boy.

I forfeit the few dollars in my pocket to buy the Saturday paper from a book stall. I read as I amble on to the Africa Freedom Park along Second Street.

The news gives me that "not-yet-uhuru" feeling: weird things are happening around the world, people eating each other, lovers killing each other, leaders threatening each other with war, women and children dying in war-torn zones.

I sit on a bench and carry on poring over my newspaper. A man, dry-lipped, and frail, comes to sit on the same bench with me. The bold bar-line on the centre fold reads, "Bakers Increase Price of Bread by 1000%." And a certain story is captioned "Fuel price skyrocket as supply dwindles".

The man cranes his head to read the headline also, and then he shakes his head and says, "A time is coming when we will pay for goods with our lives, not with money. Corruption will cut the leaders away from the people in Africa. Power will corrode communication. Violence will be the only dish of hot soup hurled upon an already poor people. The violence will come in the form of abnormal price hikes, and the empty gimmicks that try to justify the doings of unscrupulous fathers who abuse power to the detriment of the masses. Look over there."

The man points to a crowd upbeat about a battle between a vendor and the municipal police. Ten municipal policemen are beating up a vendor with batter sticks and hell-sent kicks. The vendor, a youth, tries to run away but he is grabbed by the belt, and his back is slashed and chopped by batter sticks as fruits and cigarettes scatter all over the dirty tarmac. They throw the young man into the back of their van, which is cramped with seized fruits, vegetables, and other vendors. The women who are illegally selling cell phone re-charge cards on another street corner try to run away but are captured and thrown into the van, which heads towards the Town House. The man beside me walks away silently.

As I leave the Park, a young woman with the face of Africa looks at me... The face, oval, glinting, kind, and intelligent, summarises all about her and there are no loose ends whatsoever. She walks by and disappears without a backward glance. Memories of the woman from the bus; the angel who gave up her seat for me flash back in my mind. Anyway, I fold my paper and head southwards to the heavy industries where I hope to spend the rest of the day playing draughts with other redundant men.

Beaven Tapureta is a zestful creative writer, journalist, poet, and founder of Writers International Network Zimbabwe. He was nominated for the NAMA 2009, and is working on a novel.

Lost Love

Lost Love

Ivor W. Hartmann

Valentine's, that damn day of year when he remembers her most vividly. They, *the sea of strangers who washed through this his last home before the box.* They *hung up unsightly decorations around the ward. Big, fat and fluffy hearts stringed like impaled limbless teddy bears. He tried to ignore it all by rolling his aching bones and looking out at the dull day outside the windows. But she he could not ignore, nor forget, not today.*

She is a haunting that reminds his heart it was she, it had always been, since he was sixteen. Life conspired to keep them apart; even the close friendship they once had faded away, driven into nothing by time, distance, and her other men's arms. She was a glorious butterfly whose wings unfolded too soon for him to behold and protect. Her wings took her into hands that bruised and crushed her spirit in their haste to capture her virginal soul. But he knew, he knew who she was, he saw, he saw who she was, that bright and blinding inner core, which no force on this earth could ever touch.

She was a brilliant and rare orchid that grew in-between jagged skeletons of rusted junkyard cars, birthed from foul ground soaked in oil, sweat, blood, semen, lies, betrayals and desperation. From these jaded beginnings she somehow grew in opposite, in defiance, in spite of, into the heavenly creature he saw first in a darkened lair; stale beer, cheap cigarettes, bad music and plenty of so-fuelled blind testosterone with no perceived outlet but sex and/or violence.

He was jacked that night with a new heady brew of spliff, wino-sherry and surging hormones. But when he saw her, it dropped away to barely a blip and time coalesced into an endless vision.

She danced alone with her eyes closed and seemed to move to a beat more powerful than what ears alone could hear. Where others rocked and gyrated, grinding into each other as if trying to meld their bodies, she danced alone. Where others spun wildly careening off the tight-packed crowd around them, she alone had a solid metre of inviolable space. Men would bounce their way inside but just as quickly bounce out, repelled by forces unseen, all the while her eyes remaining closed. She danced for herself. She danced to cast out the demons that coiled around them all. She danced for her life and unfurled those wings that took her soul beyond this reality. Beyond this infinitesimal fraction of dimension, time and space. He knew that to enter that space and remain, he would need the utmost conviction and the deepest good intentions. Nothing else would do.

His was a small town and soon as he grew his associations outward, there she was a shining teenage star who held a considerable entourage fixed around her orbit. The music came first, it always seemed to then, music to try and classify your teenage-self. To claim your membership to something that divided you from them, and so defined you. They, both cool as Siamese cats, swapped music at the end of the night they officially met, before they had said more than one word in a row to each other. When they met up again it was with a new-found respect, and the monosyllables broke rank into a real conversation. A beginning that was an end was never truer than that moment of connection-.

Lost Love

Here They *come again, it's bath-time again. How he wishes* They *would just leave him in smelly peace. He nearly remembers this one's name, something like Petula. As she hefts him into sitting he squints at her name tag, Nurse Beulah. He wonders for an instant if nurse is her first name, then fumes over this modern "first names only because it's more friendly" business. Damn it, he didn't get this old only to be called by his first name. Trouble was he couldn't at that moment remember his own name either. The nurse starts humming something while wiping his back and a voice sings out in his mind.*

She sang, and when she sang it felt like the universe had ceased and only her voice and he remained, alone in an endless blackness. The voice of an angel that lived within her, that was her, that only came out in brief moments which stopped time. How he wanted the world to hear what he heard, and yet he wanted it only for himself too, his singing angel. Instead, her audience sat in endless, jam-packed, vomit-soaked cars; they were always going somewhere yet seemingly nowhere, some house, some club, some river, some place, all fixed by a nowhere ring of familiar faces. She was the nowhere anchor with a golden voice that rang out clear above blown-speaker wailings. In dank garages converted to teenage caves of freedom, her voice whispered lullabies to the comatose. In hallucinogen depths, lost and bewildered, as the world cried out in mutual agony, her voice carried on the wind, a rock of certain balm that soothed the pounded-thin raw bleeding mind.

But the moment, their moment, their time to be together never arrived, always a potential, never an expression. First, she was partnered, and then he when she became free. So the die was set, a lifetime of inopportune moments.

African Roar

It's lunchtime. They *sling trays of the usual, whatever bland and overcooked. He quickly forces it all down mechanically even though he has no appetite; it's not worth the trouble from* Them *if he doesn't. He lies back down and turns to the windows, trying to ignore the incessant love songs that whimper through the ward from some damn radio. He needs no more reminders today; his memories of her are more real than the ward already.*

There was one occasion, one moment, one exception that proved the rule in their intangible life-long ghost affair. Three days he had between a real messy separation and forced perusal of a new career in foreign lands. Three days they were, for the first time in eleven years, both single. Three days that could have been the beginning.

It should have started with a kiss, they had kissed before, one drunken, cloak-room moment years ago that they both enjoyed. A stolen moment they never talked about, except as a fond but whispered slightly guilty pleasure — they were both with other people at the time.

As their children from other people played happily together in the garden, they watched, and sipped sweet tea in the shade, chatting amiably. There was a subtle tension between them he had not felt before. He finally realised here was a time, a space, a conglomeration of events that had conspired and enabled that mutually long-hauled potential to be explored. She asked if he would like to stay the night, with a gleam in her eyes that told him she had realised too. He just smiled and nodded in agreement, not daring to expose the quiver he knew his voice would have.

Finally, when their kids were headlong into their own dreams, they retired to her bedroom to watch a movie. They lay close, millimetres only between their shoulders. But life colluded against him as it dangled the ultimate fruit only to cut his balls off at the same time, for the first time. Try as he might he could not get the spark of desire to flare, he silently begged all the gods and goddesses in existence, ever, to show him some mercy just the merest twitch of life to indicate the slimmest possibility of an erection. He begged and pleaded in vain. The Kiss was not kissed, the fire was not started, and a new beginning was lost. She politely fell asleep and he soon joined her, but did wake up in time to see the dawn grace her immaculate sleeping form. Just before her child woke her up and she hurried off into the day's schedule, as did he.

He left town and they never saw each other again, their country collapsed into economic chaos, she fled to the great isles beyond the sea and he... He jumped in the Atlantic Ocean naked once, just to be in the freezing same waters that crashed on her far removed shores-.

A loud weeping interrupts his reverie. Damn it all, did everyone wear their hearts on their sleeve now, what happened to public emotional control, he blustered silently. Peering around the ward to spot the bastard, he saw no offenders. One of the nurses stared at him from her station obviously annoyed as he was at the blubberer, yet she continued the stare only at him. It was then he felt the tears on his face and the shuddering gasps of breath between loud sobs. He's so shocked it ripples through his body like an electric charge and the weeping cuts off mid sob. He lies down mortified, yet dives once more into his remaining memories of her.

Over the decades the phone calls dwindled to emails, emails to sms's, to sms's only on special occasions, and then one year to nothing at all. Yet hope, faintest hope, hope which considers a possibility of lifetimes of which this one is but a part, remained with him. It made no sense but she still occupied his heart. A presence that still talked back with a sparkle in her eyes and hinted an understanding of goddess like proportions; one which always asked him to be godlike too, to be gods together as they were intended to be.

She called, one last time, a few months before cancer took her away. They talked for hours, reminisced about old times, and just for a moment time stood still when she sang for him one last time. Her honeyed voice the world never did get to hear, apart from a few lost backyard studio sessions. No doubt, gathering dust in someone's basement along with all the other mislaid dreams of youth. She laughed afterwards, in that same laugh from long ago, a laugh still free from life's scars. They said goodbye like they always did, as though they still lived near and would drop in unannounced sometime later that day.

He listens for her voice among the thousand sounds that indicate dinner is near. It's a hope that when he hears her it will be time to finally leave his old bones to questing roots. To fly free, as they both spread their wings and soar away, together at last. He doesn't know what makes him think she has waited, but he listens with all his heart anyway.

Ivor W. Hartmann, co-editor of *African Roar,* is a Zimbabwean writer, visual artist and editor/publisher of the *StoryTime* ezine. Currently based in Johannesburg, South Africa he has published numerous short stories, essays and reviews in print and online literary magazines. In 2009, he was nominated for the UMA Award, and awarded The Baobab Prize. He is currently working on a collection and a novel.

A Cicada in the Shimmer

Christopher Mlalazi

It was trapped inside his mind, which was a world falling away into a darkish-greyish, shimmering soot. He opened his eyes. Pale light shafted into the room through a rent in the curtain, but, groggily, he knew that it was a moon beam, and it was still night.

He turned inside the blankets onto his left and removed the heels of his palms digging into his ears. The trill was still there, incessant, and now outside his head. He ground his palms over his ears again, tightly. The sound pierced on, now inside his head again.

He stared in sleepy thought at the dark smudge of the ceiling. Had the cicada drilled into the soil of his mind and lodged there? He screwed his eyes shut and tried to see inside his mind. Nothing visible there, except for the indistinct and formless shimmers. Silver algae floating on a black pool? Black itches on a silver skin? Or was that the form life assumed inside itself? Could he identify the pestering cicada and banish it from in there with a single concentrated thought? And if he failed, was it going to eat his brains and make them mushy, just as his mother said it did to bad people? But Suku had been the one who had showed him her little fist with the tip of her thumb protruding from between the pointing and middle fingers as they prepared to hide; then she had taken his hand and led him into the dark maize field behind Dumi's home.

"Can we come?" Dumi's voice had called from around the house.

"Not yet!" Suku had called back - from underneath him.

They were fully clothed and enfolded in the secrecy of the arms of the night. Even the faint orange light from a distant tower-light failed to penetrate into the field. He had felt the hands of the darkness pulling his head down, its warm breath, its wet lips, and he had wrenched himself free and fled away towards the house, a premonition of dread washing over him. Something had missed his head from behind, as he ran, and fallen in front of him. He had looked down. It was a maize cob. He had rounded the house, and a bulky shadow was standing in the veranda.

"CAN WE COME?" Dumi's voice had called out from the shadow - then the shadow leapt into two shadows and Dumi's voice continued from one of them. "What are you doing here Jemusi?"

"I am going home to eat," Jemusi had replied, a tremor in his voice.

"That's not fair!" the other shadow had wailed in a girl's voice.

"Beatrice is right," Dumi's shadow had said again. It sounded angry. "Give us a chance to find you and then hide also. You and Suku can't do it alone."

But Jemusi had walked away into the night, just as Suku emerged from around the corner of the house behind him. In her hand she held a maize cob. She had raised it into a throwing position, aiming for Jemusi's back, but then her hand had dropped to her side again without launching the missile. There was a pout on her lips.

A tiny mosquito hovered over him, its whine that of ten of them. He swatted at it, missed, but the moonbeam gulped it down. In the cocoon of the blankets that came up to his ears, he closed his eyes and tried to count the sounds of the cicadas trilling away – were they in his mind or outside it? They sounded like two, one steady and the other intermittent. Husband and wife weeping at the scarcity of bread and meat from shops – oh, how he wanted to sleep! He was tired of not being able to, no matter how much he closed his eyes and tried to wish himself to do so. And he also could not sit up in the darkness. He was afraid of the ogres from his mother's tales, that they would abduct him and take him far, where they would cook and eat him bones and all. Why had he agreed to hide with Suku in the first place? He could have chosen Dumi, and the cicadas would have left him in peace...

When he had got home after deserting the hide and seek game, his mother had been cooking at the fire.

"Food is not yet ready," maDube had told him. Their two-roomed home squatted behind her, as if contemplating the dark night. "They sold me wet wood and it is not burning - the thieves. They need reporting to *murambatsvina* and have their wood shop burnt to the ground!" She spat in disgust as smoke writhed past her face and raced for the stars.

"I need water to bathe," Jemusi had said, sitting on a brick by the fireside, his back to the house, his eyes on two pots on the fire. The pots seemed to be grinning at him. Burning and grinning. A woman was screaming somewhere in the womb of the night.

"Move back!" maDube had snapped. "Can't you see the pot is boiling? You want to get me into trouble with your father when you get scalded like that woman who is being killed by her husband?"

She had cocked her ear into the night.

"Hear!"

The screaming had become hoarse, as if the woman was now being strangled.

He had moved back. His mother's hands were unpredictable, especially the left one, the one least expected because she was right handed.

"What was that about water?" she had asked him as she prodded the fire with a stick.

"I want to bathe," Jemusi had repeated.

"Woooo! What is the moon hearing tonight!" she had exclaimed. "Say it again my child."

"I want to bathe," he had whispered, one eye on the moon, the other on his mother.

The night had stirred, and the fire had crackled and spat colourful sparks at it.

"Listen to this child," maDube had said, stirring inside one of the pots with a pestle. "Last night I called you to come and bathe and you cried and ran away to play hide and seek with Suku, who bathes everyday before the sun has set whilst you roll in dust like a goat. What do you want to wash with water that you can't wash with dust, heh? What have you been doing with Suku anyway? Or you have gone back to maDloldo?"

MaDloldo was Dumi's grandmother, and lived two houses away from Dumi's home in her own house. It was whispered by adults, usually at night and in the safety of locked houses, that she was a witch and that was why Dumi's father and mother had died as thin as grass because she wanted them to become her new goblins because the ones she had, had expired.

"Aaah mama!"

"Where are we going to get cows for the dowry my son when your father doesn't even own a grasshopper? Tell me that?"

"Aaaah mama! I am not married."

"Then why do you want to bathe when you are just about to go to sleep when you are not married?"

"I last bathed days ago, I am now smelling," he had said, tears moistening the corners of his eyes, and fear gripping his heart. Had his mother smelt Suku on him? Why all this talk about marriage?

"Bathing tomorrow won't make a difference," she had promptly declared, and then pointed at a tin full of water warming beside the fire. "That water is your father's when he comes in from the beer-garden, you know what he sells there and he cannot sleep with its smells. Ants would eat him and your witch maDlodlo would have no father in-law."

"I want to bathe!" Jemusi had cried out.

His mother had snatched a burning log from the fire, and he had fallen silent. She had poked the log back into the fire again, sending more sparks leaping.

Another mosquito, this one so big it almost filled the room, appeared over him. It flew on silent wings. The trill in his mind was now flying above the moon. The mosquito stared at him, its wings silver blurs.

"Weeeee-" it said in a voiceless voice, smiling. "It's eating your mind isn't it?"

"Take it away please!" Jemusi cried out from his blankets, the heels of his palms still grinding into both of his ears.

The mosquito winked, and, magically, the trill disappeared from his mind. He removed his palms from his ears. The mosquito was trilling, the same trill that had been bothering him inside his mind. He suddenly felt relaxed. He smiled. The world felt blissful. The mosquito dived. He swatted with his hand. There was a sting on his neck, and the mosquito was hovering over him again, its body shot through by a moon beam. Its stomach bulged with blood. He recognised the blood. It was his! He swatted again with his hand. The mosquito jinked, and it was hovering over him yet again, now wearing red boxing gloves. He opened his mouth to shout at it, and it squirted a bucket-full of blood into it.

"A taste of your own blood." It grinned at him as he chocked.

He jerked upright from the blankets, bile rushing up his intestines.

"Blood!" he thought, aghast, and the surge of bile halted at his throat. His mouth was wide open, and he expected to see the bile jet out and bloody the room. A drop of saliva yo-yoed from the tip of his bottom lip to his lap. He was gasping, tears blurring his sight. He felt the bile subside.

A finger knocked on the back of his head. He looked up. The mosquito was no longer there. Several moon beams now criss-crossed the room, also searching for the mosquito. The finger knocked on the back of his head again. He looked further up, and the finger flicked into his throat, making him jerk his chin down onto his chest...

He was walking along an avenue of maize plants, his chin still stuck to his chest. Silver moonlight radiated from him upwards. He was walking through the silver shimmers. Ahead, the orb of the earth glowed a filthy dark green.

A foot in a goatskin sandal suddenly flashed and stamped the earth to a speck of dust.

"Too much trouble," a familiar voice growled, blowing the dust away. Jemusi looked up, surprised, but his chin was stuck fast to his chest. He looked sideways. It was his father Mathiya, dressed in blood spattered white overalls, and smelling of goat meat. They both sneezed as some of the crushed earth dust got into their noses.

"And too much stink," said Jemusi, his nose puckered.

They were communicating telepathically.

"Sometimes I wonder if it is inherent in me." A worried frown creased Mathiya's chin.

Earthen gourds, brimming with goat blood, appeared in their hands. Mathiya poured libation to the ground and they drank.

"You should not have given them sexual organs," Jemusi said after a short pause.

"Honestly, I could not think of any other exciting way they could break the boredom of hide and seek, son."

There was a guffaw. They looked up. MaDlodo stood in mid air above them, dressed in a voluminous white dress.

A Cicada in the Shimmer

"I have always warned you not to mix drink with work, Mathiya and son," maDlodlo said in a cracking voice, then guffawed.

MaDlodlo was not well versed in telepathy, and her voice constantly broke out of the element, agitating the shimmers, and making them swirl.

"Look at what always happens to your children – weeeee in their heads." She guffawed again.

She had a beautiful but very old face, and the tail of a snake swished behind her.

"Shut up!" Mathiya said.

The tail curled, and its tip jabbed towards Mathiya, making Jemusi jump back in alarm. The smell of snuff hung on the still air.

"You have failed in all your endeavours, and I have always succeeded in all of mine," MaDlodlo said, now the crack gone from her voice and leaving it sweet sounding. "Did you smell the lovely stink from the overflowing mortuaries from my last trick before you scrunched that dot you call earth under your sandal?"

"You are a witch," spat Mathiya.

"My my, such ugly words from my father-in-law." She pointed a finger at Mathiya. "And point of correction, I am not a witch doctor, but a traditional one. I keenly await your next divinely inspired creation, lord Mathiya, and, to make the game more interesting, a tip for you."

MaDlodlo looked up and opened her mouth wide. A firestorm violently twisted out of it. It exploded into the void above them, roaring, whirling viciously. Jemusi and his father watched open mouthed, the now mushroom shaped firestorm reflected in their eyes. MaDlodlo's cheeks were smiling. The mushroom head suddenly convulsed into the words "NORTH KOREA," and collapsed back into her mouth.

MaDlodlo twisted her right cheek up at them. "Ooh, so lovely!"

She became a cicada, which, in mid air, trilled once and disintegrated into a shimmer.

"She is mad," Jemusi said.

Mathiya shrugged his shoulders, and spat a new earth into his hand. He tossed it into space and it hung suspended above them.

"Again?" asked Jemusi.

Mathiya nodded his head sagely. "I have to discover where I always go wrong, for my creations are me."

Mathiya took a knife, then cut off the tit of his right breast. He breathed on it, and it became another Jemusi. He placed him on the airborne earth.

"Maybe you should have made a woman first," Jemusi advised in a whisper, eyeing his replica critically. "That one has a cicada in his head."

"Next time if this one goes wrong too," Mathiya whispered back, and then he clapped his hands once, and the cosmos lit up around the earth, iridescent. Mathiya closed his eyes, and his voice broke out of telepathy.

"Let it begin," he gave the order.

Jemusi watched as the glowing universe started revolving, making a trilling sound, just like the Humber bicycle his father rode when he went to sell goat meat at the beer-garden. A cicada emerged from a shimmer and raced towards Jemusi's ear. He grunted and jerked his chin up. It was still stuck fast to his chest. The cicada was getting nearer. He knew it wanted to get into his ear and into his mind, where it would begin its trill. He jerked his chin harder, grunting loudly, his heart thumping, but it was immovable.

"Are you okay?" his mother's voice said.

He opened his eyes and looked up. The darkness above him took her form. She was leaning over him, holding a paraffin lamp. A wrap was tied around her body.

"I am okay," Jemusi replied.

His heart felt light, and so his body too, as if he was drifting away with the world.

A Cicada in the Shimmer

"You were grunting in your sleep," his mother said. The light from the lamp made her face look gentler. "What were you carrying that was so heavy?"

"I was seeing," Jemusi said.

MaDube contemplated him for a moment, her face becoming even gentler. "What did you see tonight, my son?" she asked in a soft voice.

"The country," Jemusi's voice was drifting away.

"What of it?"

"It is a shimmer."

"What are you talking about Jemusi?"

"The shimmer is a dying cicada that refuses to give up its trill."

"And the cicada is maDlodlo!" MaDube declared vehemently. "She is a witch, but she will never get you. You must not play with her grandson Dumi, otherwise you will become him." Her voice lowered to a whisper. "How many times have I told you he is other things?"

"Many times mama," Jemusi mumbled.

His mother had once told him that Dumi flew for his grandmother at night to go and bewitch people. That he was the cat that sometimes screeched in the township at night. But Jemusi did not believe all this. He liked Dumi. He was a good person to be with, always concerned for other people.

His mother placed a warm hand over his forehead. "Go away witch," she said in a low but strong voice. "What do you want in this house? Can't you see we are not like your children whom you ate, we are poor and suffering? If it's the goats that Jemusi's father is selling, people are not buying the meat. Please leave us alone!"

A moment later, a sleepy Jemusi saw his mother sprinkling salt around the room. Then she disappeared into the bedroom, where his father's bleating snore could be heard, as it was in appeasement to the spirits of the goats he butchered and sold everyday at the beer-garden.

He had squatted for sometime besides the fire, warming his hands on it, not answering his mother who kept up a steady torrent of conversation as she cooked. The scream of the woman in the distance had now been replaced by that of a man.

"She is now killing him," his mother had commented gleefully, adding mealie meal to the sadza pot, and stirring it with agitated strokes. "Hear! Kill the dog!"

"Maybe he has killed her, how do you know?"

"Have you ever heard of soldiers grieving for the people they have killed, even if they are their own?"

"You don't know soldiers."

"I don't know soldiers? What are you saying? Don't you know your mother was living in the rural areas before and after Independence and she saw all the killings – that was before your grandfather left us this box of a house where you were born?"

"I am going to tell father when he comes," Jemusi had said.

"Tell him, this is not a house but an empty shoe box. He knows that very well."

"I am going to tell him, mama!"

"Another father is screaming," maDube had replied. "What has happened to your ears? Has the cicada got into them?"

Jemusi had sidled nearer his mother, casting fearful glances around him.

"How many times have I told you to never mention that!" An angry voice had bellowed from the corner of the house, then a bicycle had emerged from the darkness, followed by Mathiya, who was pushing it.

Jemusi had leapt up and ran to his father. Reaching him, he had grabbed his legs.

"What kind of a mother are you?" Mathiya had continued. He had leaned the bicycle against the wall, then he scooped up Jemusi into his arms.

A Cicada in the Shimmer

"Put him down," maDube said. "He is too old for that now."

"You are harming him with your insensitive talk."

"You are spoiling him too!"

Mathiya had put Jemusi down. Then he had sat on a bench and pulled Jemusi over his knee. Jemusi had placed his cheek against his father's chest. His father smelt of goat meat, which was comforting. And he was so powerful. He could hear his big heart pumping in his chest below his blood stained white overalls.

"What did you see today?" his father had asked him, his body suddenly gone tense.

"Nothing," Jemusi had replied, and he had felt his father's body relax.

"Can you kill a goat?" Mathiya had asked.

"Children don't kill goats," maDube had said. "Do you want to give him nightmares? He has enough already as it is."

"Shh," Mathiya had said. "He is sleeping. Take him into the house and give me my food. And please don't switch on the radio, it might wake him up."

"That stupid radio. All it can do is go weeeeeeee, or – Rambai makashinga when we are so hungry like this!"

Somewhere in the distance, voices had been raised in chant, accompanied by fervent drum beat – an initiation dance for spirit mediums at maDlodlo's house, Jemusi's mother knew – the witch...

African Roar

Christopher Mlalazi is the 2010 Feuchtwanger Fellow at the Villa Aurora in Pacific Palisades, California, after which he will return to his home country of Zimbabwe at the end of 2010, where he lives and writes from. He was short listed for The Nordic Africa Institute's Guest Writers Grant for 2010. He has also published two books, a short story collection *Dancing with Life: Tales from the Township* (2008), which won a National Arts Merit Award for Best First Book in 2009, and was also short listed for the 2009 NOMA award for book publishing in Africa. His second book is a novel, *Many Rivers*, which was nominated for Outstanding Fiction Book at the 2010 National Arts Merit Award.

Quarterback & Co.

Chuma Nwokolo, Jr.

2nd August, 2004

My name is George Franz. Although I am not entirely sure, I suspect that a disastrous fate has just overtaken me. I will set down the bare facts: about ten minutes ago an insect probably settled on my temple, extended its proboscis, and sucked approximately a quarter of my brains out.

To set things in proper perspective, and to remind myself, I should mention that I am an efficiency analysis manager at KwoiTech, an FTSE company that hires its management very carefully and polices their health just as solicitously. Every year we attend a two-day medical retreat at a sumptuous health farm in Gloucestershire. Mental health isn't one of the advertised categories tested, but I came to discover the identity of the nosey bloke who made cryptic notes on his paper napkins as we ate in the cafeteria, when I caught him in the john, dictating my psychiatric evaluation into a Dictaphone.

It might also be important to mention that my greatest craving within the walls of KwoiTech is for a no-holds-barred, hour-long nap. I suppose my predilection for sleep has a long history. It started back in Vietnam, more than fifteen years ago, when I got on the wrong side of a government minister and got hauled before the court on a charge so complicated that I still don't fully understand it today. However, the lawyer hired for me by KwoiTech assured me that the company and I were guilty as charged, and that I was looking at a minimum of twenty years in jail, unless I was prepared to take some radical, extra-legal steps. The first two options he suggested were too preposterous for consideration (believe me). Then he fetched a shaman who mixed me a concoction. It worked like a dream. Every time I stood up in the dock to listen to the charge, I would literally fall into the deepest sleep, a sleep so profound that even the lacerations of a whip would not rouse me. The doctors diagnosed an ominous and nameless tropical disease. After a dozen or so adjournments, the charges against me were dropped, as it was apparently unlawful to prosecute a defendant who was too ill even to plead guilty or not guilty.

Triumphantly, the lawyer took me back to his shaman for the antidote, a two-course medication dispensed on consecutive days. I drank the first dram uneventfully, but when I returned on the second day, it was to receive the apocalyptic news that the shaman had been killed by a hit-and-run bus driver. I have drunk several concoctions from several dubious purveyors since, but I am stuck with this residual and perpetual desire for a mid-day snooze. I crave siestas the way other men in my position crave affairs with their fellow workers.

Unfortunately, the corporate culture in KwoiTech considers the temporary abdication of brain function induced by sleep, when indulged within office hours, a more heinous crime than office liaisons. My seniority in the company has not earned me private offices, for even our Deputy Managing Director works from a glass-partitioned basketball-court-sized enclosure where the entire staff can observe the dexterous process of managing an FTSE company, twenty-four hours a day.

A nap might seem a simple thing, but I live in London and work in the square mile and it's not a simple thing at all. I earn £145,900 a year and work Monday to Saturday plus one Sunday a month. I get into the office at 7.45am and for the last eight months haven't left before 7pm. Even after closing, I have one-on-one, fully-expensed dinners with business prospects. Every three or four nights I wake at 3 a.m. to enter brainwaves in my notebook. Eunice is supposed to be my secretary, in reality she is my taskmistress, one of the most efficient in the entire corporate hierarchy of KwoiTech. Her diary management prowess is legendary and I have personally seen the avaricious envy on the face of my GMD, Meadows, when he passes her door.

I'd consider giving up the £45,900.00 on my salary for the opportunity to sleep an hour a day at noon, six days a week, but this is a culture where I've worked nineteen years, and it is considered disloyal to draw a lunch break unless there's a fee-paying, working-lunch appointment to tag onto it.

So, this is the 2nd of August and I have been scheming my siesta for eight days, ever since the Medilang representative cancelled his hour-long consultative meeting in my office. At this exploratory stage, the meeting wasn't a fee-earner and I'm not expected to send a fee-note afterwards. I saw the potentials of that hour right away. Eunice had popped out for a courier and his call bounced straight to my desk. It was done in seconds: a meeting cancellation that Eunice didn't know of.

Eunice.

A rare bird, a £67,860 per annum, 44-year-old staff whose job-description was secretary, but whose clout and savoir faire embarrassed youngsters on twice her salary. On her turf, even Mark Meadows did not dare confront her. Inch-for-inch, she has a larger office than either myself or Carl Bean, the Out-Sourcing Director whose diary she also polices, although that territory does include her reception space.

An hour's nap on company time.

African Roar

The dimensions of the transgression were so colossal that it did not fully form in my mind immediately. This could lead to the sort of termination that would continue to reverberate at annual Christmas parties years down the line. Up till this morning, I could still have called Eunice and confessed the hour-long hole in my diary. It would be immediately filled of course. An efficiency company like KwoiTech could right a five-hour diary dislocation in five minutes. We sell a patent-pending software that does just that to clients, but in-house, we have staff like Eunice. Yet, the temptation was too strong, At 9 a.m. today, I stepped out of my office and filled a coffee cup from the dispenser near Eunice. She was working on a spreadsheet, the half-inch nails on her little fingers tapping impatient staccatos at the microsecond delays that her TFT indulged in serving up her updated views.

"I believe Khan from Medilang is already in Conference Room 3," I said casually. I poured another cup for my 'client'.

"That's strange, he didn't stop here."

"He's been to CR3 before."

"I'll send up a pool secretary…"

"Not necessary this time…"

"You've got your Dictaphone?"

"I won't be needing it – mostly exploratory talks at this stage... Please field all my calls…"

Then I escaped. CR3 was next to the library. Naturally it has glass walls as well, but there's a nine-foot blind spot where the Library's high shelves and CR3's bank of cabinets meet. By locking the door and putting an executive chair in the blind spot I had a private space secure from all except telescopic lenses from the offices across the street. I put the coffee cups down, switched off my mobile phone and set my watch to wake me up in sixty minutes. I also opened the window for some fresh air: my one, grievous mistake, and within seconds after I let myself go, I was sleeping soundly.

Until I was woken up fifty minutes later, by the insect bite which cost me a quarter of my brains.

I understand how all this might distress the more squeamish of my readers. Perhaps such readers will also imagine how harrowing it must be for me. At the moment, my own sympathies are required closer to home. I woke up in CR3 expecting to feel more rested than I had ever felt in years, instead, I felt light-headed and distinctly unwell. There was a small weal on my temple, which I could discern with my right index finger; nothing dramatic, nothing that felt like the tunnelling site of a major evacuation, but inside, a major headache was brewing. It was not quite 10 a.m. and my alarm had not beeped. I could hear a resonant buzz, and my quartz watch did not do buzzes. A movement snapped my head in the direction of the sound, towards the open window, as the buzz faded away.

Now, I'm back on my desk, no longer positive that it was an insect that woke me up. I'm not even certain it was an insect that sucked a quarter of my brains out. When I first woke up I was terribly certain... but an hour has passed, I am back on my desk, and in the interests of my continued tenure on this job, I'm not as sure as I was...

I got off the chair and activated my phone. I pulled another coffee from the dispenser. It was when I tried to recall my next appointment that I became convinced that something was desperately wrong. For the life of me, I couldn't recall the entry on my diary for 10.10 a.m.

That knocked me down flat. I usually recall my diary minutiae a week in advance. I nervously fingered the weal on the side of my head. I shook my head, hating the bounce as the remnants of my most important organ acquainted itself with the extra space in its accommodation. I had a sudden mental picture of an insect sinking a proboscis into the centre of my skull, and sucking and sucking until I woke in the nick of time to save, what?... perhaps three quarters of my brain function.

I suppose I ought to just own up and quit. Normally I have to throw in a hundred and twelve percent just to stay on top of this job. To attempt to keep it as a half-wit, (or more accurately, three-quarter-wit) would be the height of presumption. The modality will present a problem of course. I cannot be honest with Mark, or anyone else, about the reasons for my sudden resignation. There will be no sense in having a posse of psychiatric nurses chasing after me on the underground. Then there's the problem of the mortgage. If I cannot keep this job, I certainly can't interview for another one in the city; and the wages in window cleaning won't pay for my pad. Perhaps I can discuss the possibility of a job share with Mark: I could work full-time and only earn three-quarters of my salary, with the balance of my wages set aside for a personal assistant to follow after me with post-it notes in the capacity of a Deputising Memory...

I managed to get through the rest of the day without major incident, spending most of my time feeling around my memory to figure out what was lost and what was left. Thankfully enough – if there's anything to be thankful about in this catastrophe – none of my motor functions seemed to have been lost, so I can walk and talk without any hint of the bizarre disaster that has just befallen me.

Now here I am back home, really feeling sorry for myself. This job makes nutcases of the best of men. The other day Ellis returned from his business trip to Punjab. He went for a Systems Audit of a plantation client of ours that harvests and processes sugar. He toiled a stressful week among the vats of molasses, spending with his nights in a crummy hotel with only a flimsy door between him and the temperamental charges of an itinerant snake charmer, who daily plied his art at the hotel entrance. So

Quarterback & Co.

Ellis came back from India and missed his first morning at work – a sackable offence at KwoiTech. Come afternoon, we got a mobile call from a distressed client who recognised Ellis sitting cross-legged near the escalator at the Bond Street underground station, fluting for a bucket of earthworms in the best impression of a snake-charmer that was possible without a snake.

This was the depressed trajectory of my thoughts when I heard a distinct buzzing, the sort of sound a really big bee would make. I looked around my living room, but there was nothing remotely bee-like flying around. I walked carefully through the flat, looking apprehensively into every closet for a trapped bee, or wasp, then I turned the corner into my study and saw it.

It was buzzing over my notebook. I'm not going to say what I thought it was doing. I know how the Mental Health Act works; and I know people who have been too honest about their thoughts and observations that have had their entire lives hijacked by the psychiatric process. So I won't say what I suspect. I will simply state what I saw: this really big bee-like organism buzzing slowly over my notebook; buzzing, that is to say, from left to right, parallel to the lines, as though it were reading them (which of course it was not doing, as even madmen know that bees don't read).

I suppose some of my readers are well acquainted with the academic bees of Southern Antigua, which have been observed in the wild performing similar acts on discarded newspapers caught in thorn bushes, but the really neat thing about this bee-like organism (which I decided to christen Quarterback) was that as it buzzed along the lines of my notebook, I gained an incredibly graphic image of the writings on the page. It was... how shall I say this safely (in the light of the Mental Health Act)... almost as though Quarterback were an extension of my mental faculties. To translate this phenomenon into computer-speak, it was as though Q were a scanning device relaying data to my central processor by radio waves.

I developed a strange affinity with Quarterback over the next few days. My initial desire to imprison it in an empty jam jar proved unnecessary. It went everywhere with me. What was even more uncanny was the fact that Q was audible but invisible. It was also something of a stalker. The other day it chose to dog Eunice. She complained of a buzzing in her head, although she could not see Q hovering, literally right above her cleavage.

7th March, 2005

My fears concerning my mortgage proved unfounded. Indeed, I have since moved twice, and the premises I currently occupy come with a kidney-shaped swimming pool and floodlit lawn tennis court, much to the envy of my colleagues at work. Unfortunately, such is my schedule at KwoiTech that I am yet to audition any of these facilities, six weeks after moving in. My career has literally taken off. Indeed, back in December, Eunice warned the KwoiTech board of the headhunting proposals jamming my email inboxes and three desperate board directors took me off on a riotous Florida weekend in the course of which they plied me with flattery and stock options until I signed the first three-year-contract in KwoiTech history. I am now considered KwoiTech's most important human resource. Eunice has been withdrawn from dual utility, and charged with the fierce responsibility of protecting me from poachers. I am not bothered with the pedestrian assignments that bedevil the lives of the company's middle level talent stream. I am brought in only at crucial tendering conferences where corporate fortunes are made and lost. My ability to predict the competition's figures to the broken penny has entered industry legend. And the mechanical buzzing that accompanies me has led to the sore-losers' pub gossip peddled by our poo-faced competition that I am a patent-pending robotic android invented by a KwoiTech client.

Which is all well and good, but the biggest benefit for me is the fact that I am now able to indulge daily hour-long siestas. Between noon and 4 pm Eunice arranges domestic stuff for me to do in the office. Quarterback takes that opportunity to settle by my mobile phone (it just loves my ringtone) for a sumptuous snooze. While I'm puttering around the office, Quarterback steals a four-hour siesta. Do the math! By the time it is time for my next critical conference, Q is ready to go.

3rd June, 2005

This is the end.

I've got to be fast.

Guess who my Vietnamese visitor last week was.

Yes, the lawyer who got my charges dropped. I took him for a drink in a cocktails bar.

"Still remember that shaman who died?" he asked.

"Sure," I said.

"Well, here's the authentic antidote."

"Go on!" I joked, "Did he mail it in from the dead?"

"Well it did come by mail, but it was from the executor of the estate of the dead shaman."

At this moment, Quarterback was stalking a man wreathed in mists of cannabis. So, in my favour, it must be argued that I was not in possession of all my faculties. I knocked back the concoction. I was thinking how much more productive I could be without that four-hour hiatus in the middle of my working day. As it transpired, I thought wrong. I set down the bottle. Quarterback fell to the carpet, with a terminal-sounding type of thud. I followed soon afterwards.

Turns out the potion had a 'best-before' date.

African Roar

I'm out of hospital now. I'm afraid Quarterback wasn't so lucky. I now have to sleep twenty-two hours daily. So I cannot be too far away from bed. KwoiTech took me through every specialist on Harley Street. Then they retired me. (Very reluctantly: news of my disengagement shaved a nasty seventeen percent off the company's share price.) Still, a three-year contract was a three-year contract. (And it was their lawyer who drugged me). So they paid dearly.

I don't have enough time to work anymore.

Or to write long paragraphs.

Or sentences.

But I do swim the kidney-shaped pool. In ten-minute sessions.

Chuma Nwokolo, Jr. is an author and attorney. Called to the Bar in 1985, his calling to writing was somewhat earlier, having published his first novel with Macmillan in 1983. He has a passion for the short story and his *African Tales at Jailpoint* (Villagerhouse) appeared in 1999. He has published four novels, a short story anthology, a collection of essays, and a poetry collection. Married with four children, he divides his time between the UK and Nigeria.

A Return to the Moonlight

Emmanuel Sigauke

When my brother Ranga and his wife arrived on Sunday, they roused the village with their car, which bounced as it entered the compound and came to a dignified stop in the shade of our Muzeze tree. A car in our home! Mai and I would have embraced and patted it, but, as the villagers began to arrive, we rushed to greet its owners first. Ranga walked hesitantly as if he was lost, grinning and staring at everyone stolidly, mumbling his greetings. I had expected him to act differently, but not to mumble like exile had stolen his Karanga. His wife was different though — she embraced people, or rather fell into their outstretched arms, shouting, cooing, and singing her words. She locked Mai in a long embrace, and when she proceeded to greet me, she switched to English, which I appreciated, and said, "Tete! It's you, I know!" Yes, I was, but before I could confirm, in English, she added, with an Ndebele accent, "I am Nomathamsanqa, but just call me Noma. I have heard a lot about you." When I broke free from her embrace, I proceeded to my brother, who suddenly extended his hand to greet me like a stranger. I pushed that hand away and hugged him tightly; then I released him so he could greet Mai, and by the time he reached her, she was in tears. I felt my eyes burning too, but I was not about to cry in front of all these people.

African Roar

I had expected to see a car, but not the big-wheeled black Jeep that roared into Mototi. Other returning sons and daughters of the village would have driven too, but not in cars half as good as this one. Out of all the village sons and daughters in the Diaspora, my brother was the only one who lived in America. The rest were either in South Africa or Botswana, and they often rattled back into the village in beaten-up Hondas and Toyotas. As Mai and I ululated, more villagers descended on our compound. They crowded around the Jeep, talked to it, and ran away from it as they spotted its owners. Once they greeted them, they joined in our ululation and dancing. We stayed under the tree until, about an hour later, the last villager walked away; then we sat in front of the one house on our compound.

I had been looking forward to meeting the wife, the woman who had finally put some sense into my brother. She wasn't that bad-looking. If her lips had not been too thick, and her eyes not too big, she would have been a perfect beauty. Her light complexion made Ranga, standing next to her, appear like he had rolled over and over in a pool of tar. Many years in America had not done much to lighten my poor brother's complexion. He was just as dark as I who had never set foot in anybody's country; but the wife seemed to make up for the lightness we all lacked. She wore a green floral dress and matching green tennis shoes, but what was a wonder to behold were her waist-long brown braids. Even I could use braids like that on my rural head.

She laughed at everything we said, short, pointless chuckles nervous or shy people often give. No wonder she had ended up with my brother, whose other name might as well be Shyness. They seemed like a perfect match, and they fascinated me, the wife with her little laughs and the husband with his hesitant walk. Mai seemed equally fascinated, perhaps a bit disappointed at Ranga, but she liked the wife's laughter and encouraged it.

A Return to Moonlight

I knew the laughing would not last. There was a lot to talk about and to disagree on. Earlier, when we were entering the compound, she had looked at the house and crunched her face as if she was in pain. That's the moment I had been waiting for, the first reaction, Ranga's first moment of embarrassment on seeing the condition of the house, how it sat there, roofless, welcoming them with it bareness. Of course, we would come to the matter of the house later, so I steered their attention elsewhere. I talked about the weather, about how we were lucky that the rains had delayed this year, but before we connected rains to roofless houses, the wife started handing us the gifts they had brought: clothes, groceries, more clothes.

Mai and I ululated some more, but someone had to say something in English, so I said, "Thank you a million; thank you for your generosity."

The wife told me not to worry about it, adding that I was welcome, then realising that I had tricked her into speaking in English, and switching back to Karanga, she told me that it was nothing, just a little something for Mai and me. I kept thanking her nevertheless, telling her to thank Ranga for us, even though he sat there either nodding or dozing.

The quantity of the groceries worried me a little; it didn't seem like it would last for three weeks. This was disappointing. I looked at Mai and noticed that she looked disappointed too, although she was struggling not to show it. I didn't know what to say, other than continuing to thank them; it wasn't as if I could tell them they should have done a better job on groceries. Maybe they were planning to leave the rest in cash, which was a better option because Mai and I would spend the money as we wished. I liked that, and I knew Mai did too. I smiled on the prospect of more cash, smiled in the direction of Mai so she would smile too. It wasn't like we could really do anything about it, except receive what was put in front of us, so my clapping got louder and I broke into another wave of ululation.

African Roar

We were not greedy or anything, but it was high time people saw that my brother had spent many years overseas for a good reason. They didn't have to know about all of the letters he had sent us, about how he had said life in America was difficult, how in those letters he had asked repeatedly why the building of the house was taking long to complete. What mattered now, what made sense to me, what made me proud, was that he was back, finally, with a wife. With the car parked under the Muzeze tree, not just any car, but my brother's own expensive-looking Jeep, who in the village would be stupid enough to believe that he was poor?

Yes, I knew they planned to leave enough groceries to last a few weeks and enough cash to last us a long time, maybe a whole year, enough cash to cover the completion of the house. On this thought I looked at the wife, smiled and said, "You two are very kind. Thank you for thinking about us."

"This is nothing, Tete. We are the ones who should thank you for always thinking about us, for your prayers."

Oh my, prayers? I had not been inside a church, or had said a prayer in ten years, not at least since the death of my husband, but I was happy she knew we were just as important to them as they were to us. I sat there grinning, imagining that she was looking at my most appreciative face, the best I could forge, that look of village gratitude that many years of drought and dependency had trained us to show. Her face softened with compassion and she looked away.

They had done a better job with the clothes though, had brought piles and piles of new and used dresses, pairs of jeans and sweaters. I would sift through the jeans to find ones that fit me; then I would sell the rest to raise more hard currency. I knew Mai would use some of her extra clothes to pay people to work in our field.

As the wife handed us the clothes, Mai and I ululated again, but we stopped before we attracted more attention.

A Return to Moonlight

Already, Chikwari and his wife, our neighbours, had come outside of their hut and sat near their kitchen door, pretending not to be looking at us. Mai told me to sit down; then she pursed her lips and looked sideways at them. I knew her thinking was that we had to be careful not to show off. The last thing we wanted was to have people think we had suddenly become rich. Over the years, many people had suspected that we were lying when we said we had no money, and no one believed that I no longer received money for the temporary teaching job I had lost five years before. People told me I had nothing to complain about, saying, "You with a brother overseas, what problems do you have? You who was a teacher not too long ago, what do you use your pension for?" Yet the same people laughed at us because we lived in an unfinished house.

We put the gifts in one corner of the house, where our plates and pots sat underneath a cloud of flies. Mai and I had agreed to allow the couple to see those gaping pots, and the flies had cooperated by showing up in full force. We wanted someone, especially the wife, to see things as they were, and if she was like other women, if she was like how I was with my husband, she would do something about it and put some sense into her husband. I knew she had somehow influenced his return, she must have done or said something that finally made him realise that people don't just go away and disappear, but they also return home occasionally, home where your mother and sister miss you so much. And for such a healthy-looking man to let his mother live in this ruin... it was just unacceptable. He had better not say he expected me to have taken care of things. I would if I could, if I had been overseas and was the one with a university education.

He sat on his childhood stool, which Mai had kept for him all these years, and watched his wife hand us the gifts, but appeared pensive, as if he felt the pain of return. It just upset me to see him sit there like the house did not bother him. No sign of embarrassment even, just sitting there like this was the home one brought such a beautiful wife to. It was surprising that the wife had not said anything either, but maybe she was one of those women who did not confront their husbands in front of their mothers. I would have said something already.

"Mhamha and Tete, do you want me to help with anything?" the wife said. "Maybe I can wash the dishes?"

Mai and I looked at each other but quickly turned to her, and before we said anything she added, "I can start cooking too, or do anything that you want me to do?"

"Sit down, muroora," Mai said, although the wife was already sitting. "You are the guest today, let us be the ones to cook for you."

I expected my brother's wife to protest, to say she would not let us treat her like a guest, but she stretched her legs instead, and prepared to relax, as Mai had commanded.

"No, let her cook," I said. "Remember, mother, she has not prepared warm bathing water for us yet. What type of muroora forgets to do something that important?"

I waited for Mai to respond, but she just laughed, as if what I had said was not serious. Mai knew I was right. Even though we were not there when they got married, it was not too late for the wife to do what she was supposed to do for us. I looked at her, a look I knew appeared serious, and I said, "So when are you warming the water?" Before she answered, I turned to my brother and said, "Maybe he did not tell you that he has a sister and a mother?"

"Ha, iwe!" Mai protested, torching me with her disapproving look. "Let her sit. She has travelled from too far. She will boil water for us when the right time comes."

"I can do that right now," the wife said, standing up. She then looked at me and said, "You ask for warm bathing water, Tete, you get warm bathing water."

Of course, I wasn't going let her do that. Mai was right, she needed to relax.

"Sit down," I commanded and began laughing. "Listen to me, wife, sit down!"

Even Ranga twisted his lips with a smile. I knew he appreciated that I was playing my role well.

The wife sat down and said, "Your brother was right about you, Tete. You and I will get along very well."

"Would you even dare not to get along with me, Noma?" I said, immediately realising I had just used her real name, a sign that I was getting too comfortable with her.

We all laughed, Mai, the wife, and I. Ranga's smile had disappeared, and he sat silent, playing with his phone. He still looked serious, like he was doing some work. That was the Ranga I remembered, one who as a boy had always been there without being quite there, always sitting with a book in his hand, reading even where people were fighting.

I had doubted that they would enjoy themselves in the village, but they sat with us for two hours, telling us about their long drive from Harare. Honestly, all I cared to hear about was how they lived in America. I wanted to hear more about their city there, Vallejo, which they pronounced Vayeho, but Ranga kept talking about the drive from Harare, frequently interrupting the wife, who seemed to want to continue talking about "back home".

"Things there can be funny there," she said, "especially when it comes to race matters."

"Racism is everywhere, even among people of the same race," my brother said, his voice thick and authoritative. He then paused, waiting for us to pay attention to him and when he was convinced we were, he said, "Like I was saying, I was expecting more road blocks before we reached Gweru."

"You can't compare the racism among the same people with the racism of different races," the wife said, looking at me with an eye that seemed to plead for my support.

"Different ethnic groups," Ranga said, "not racial groups."

"Ethnicity is not race," the wife said. "But the point is, it took you many years to get a real job because they-."

"You don't know the reason, so keep quiet," Ranga cut in, and the wife brought her hand to her mouth, as if to cover it, but she ended up just looking at her wristwatch.

I didn't have a degree in anything but I could tell that there was something Ranga did not want Noma to say about "back home", so she gave up and listened with us as he talked about their photo stops in Kwekwe, Shurugwi, Mandava Township, and Gudo. "There is a kind of beauty in Boterekwa that I never learned to appreciate when I was younger," he said. "Doesn't the terrain remind you of some parts of the Santa Cruz, Mendocino, or many of those beautiful places of the California coastal ranges?"

The wife just shook her head and turned to hear what I was about to say.

"So, bread... of course, you eat bread there. How much does it cost in Vallejo?" I asked, pronouncing their town correctly.

Her eyes lit. "Tete, compared to here, things there are-," she began to say, but Ranga said, "We better get going." Then he stood up. "If we start now we can cover a bit of ground."

"What's this now?" I said. "You tell me you are leaving already?"

He laughed. "Just a short drive. I want to show her around." He looked at his cell phone. "We'll be done in an hour or two."

Mother looked on the ground as if she hadn't heard him, but I could tell by how she chewed her lower lip that she didn't approve.

The wife stood up too. That's when Mai reacted: "Why don't you eat first, my children?"

"I want to show your muroora my schools, so she can see where it all began."

"Where what began?" Mai said with a deep voice. "You can't just drag your wife to places without letting her rest first. Your schools don't run away."

"She wants to see where the genius germinated," he said, now playing with his wife's braids.

"Your two schools… that's a lot to see," I said. "You will need more than an hour, that's for sure."

"Well, if we also go to Magetsi to see Mako's grave." He held his chin and looked at his shoes, like that's where the grave was.

They were nice shoes.

"Will you go to Mudhomori too, to see the others — Jairos, Thandi, Tawanda?" I said, thinking that if he was on a mission to see graves, he might as well see all of them at once, and if he really wanted to see all the graves there were to see, he might as well set aside a whole day.

Ranga remained silent, looking at the hills on the east of our home like he was seeing them for the first time. The wife followed the gaze, and she too stood transfixed as if in those hills she saw her future unfolding. Ranga then shook his head and said, "All my childhood friends are gone. Gone, gone, gone."

"That's Mwari's work, what can people of flesh do about it?" Mai said, beating the ground with a small stick. "We all will go there one day."

The wife nodded her "back home" nod. Something in it said Vallejo, Vallejo, Vallejo, with the right pronunciation of it. I too would nod like that if I had braids that long. After a while she said, "It's sad, how most of our friends have died over the years. What a waste of talent."

There was a moment of silence, as if we were paying homage to the dead. I really expected the wife to protest this idea of driving around without us. How about saying "Tete and Mai, come and enjoy the car with us"? That's what a real muroora would remember to do, to put some sense into her husband.

"Well, can I come too?" I said. "I want a ride in my car."

"I don't see why not, Tete," she said. "And you are right; it's as good as your car too."

"It's my car, no doubt," I said, beating my chest.

Mai looked at me and shook her head slowly and I knew nothing would make her get in that car and go anywhere. I wanted to go, but I remembered that Mai might want a moment with me alone. I could tell she was upset already, the way she kept beating the ground with that stick.

"We'll stay to get some food ready while you two are gone." I said. "Then maybe when you come back you can give us a ride to the well."

Ranga shouted, "That's great!" and started playing with his keys.

I stood there just admiring him... no, I was not admiring him. There wasn't a lot to admire in a man who let his mother and sister live in a house like this. They could drive without us, and I didn't care that much about the ride anyway. There was more to life than rides.

"Will you take her to the river too?" I asked. "She has to see the pool of crocodiles, I am sure." I had only meant that as a joke and like an idiot he took me seriously.

"Oh, we wouldn't miss that one. She will have to see my river." He added that their last stop was Murowa, where he wanted to see the new diamond mine. Now, that was something to see for sure.

Soon as they left, I turned to Mai and said, "So what do you think?"

"I have no mouth to talk right now," she said.

"I thought you were happy your son is back. A car, a wife; what mother would not be happy?"

"A wife? Did you see me bathing in warm water here?" she said.

I laughed, but stopped immediately when I saw her face, which showed me that this was not a laughing matter.

"You laugh about poverty like its wealth. You think she is the kind of wife to stay here and help us in the fields? And did you see me being introduced to grand children?"

"Ah, don't you think she knows what she is supposed to do? She looks like a good wife. It's your son you should worry about," I said.

"I don't care what he decides to do. He is back, and she came too; that's all that I care about." After this, mother didn't want to talk about them anymore.

"So now you are upset with me too?" I asked, after she ignored a few of my questions.

Even this one was ignored too, so we worked in silence.

When they came back two hours later, their car was covered in dust and it looked more tired than they were. The wife was livelier than before, and I noticed that she was actually pretty. What had she seen in my brother whose nose sat on his face like a tired frog? He too was talking and laughing, and I thought they were now enjoying themselves and loving the idea that they were back home. It might not look like one, but our home was still a home. Even mother had loosened up and was making jokes of her own.

After dinner they announced that they were leaving.

"Ranga, you are a joker now, handiti?" I said.

"No, we have to go, Tendi. We have to."

"Driving all the way to Harare this late?" Mai said. "Why don't you sleep and wake up tomorrow?"

The wife said, "Your son got us a hotel room in Zvishavane."

Ranga nodded in agreement, and I could see Mai's face falling.

"But maiguru," I said to the wife, "you can sleep in the house here."

"Tendi, please," Ranga said, "what are you calling a house?"

110

I didn't know what to tell him at first. I dreaded the direction the conversation was about to take. I looked at him quietly, only to realise that in moments like this, my face had a way of speaking louder than words, giving away what I thought. So I said, "That's your house right there; or have you forgotten what a house looks like?" I should have just remained quiet. Now my lips were shaking. I brought my hand to my mouth.

The house sat like a ghost, roofless and door-less. But that's the house Ranga had been building for five years, sending us money that was not even enough to buy a doorframe and telling us to stretch it, to make it work. Now he was refusing to call it his house.

I was waiting to hear what mother would say. This was her chance to speak up, and she did: "We can sleep outside and you use the good room."

"Good room?" Ranga asked. "I don't see any good room here."

What we called the good room was the one with the highest walls, covered by plastic sheets on top. Yes, the good room with the clear plastic roof. At least they would be able to see the moon while they slept. "We will give up our bedroom for you, brother," I said.

"And we will sleep out here," Mai said.

I said, "There are enough rooms for everyone. We don't have to sleep outside, mother."

There was a pause, as if we were all waiting for someone who wasn't there to say the next thing. Then I saw the wife tilting her head towards me and I thought, yes, let's hear what you have to say, wife of my brother. Our *muroora* from Vallejo by way of Gwanda.

"It's not about the house, Tete," she said. "We could even camp outside too." She looked around as if to examine the quality of the outside she was talking about. "Or better, we can all sleep in the car."

"So was he joking when he said you are driving back to Zvishavane?" I asked, now looking at my brother, who was checking his jacket pockets for something, maybe his phone, or the thin music thing he had shown us, his Eye Pod.

When he found his phone he said, "We have plans."

The silence that came after his words had to be allowed to mature. I could not trust what was about to come out of my mouth, so I bit my lips. Mai looked away, and the wife opened her mouth, but said nothing.

"I need electricity for my laptop and we have phones that need to be charged," said my mother's son.

I could feel a lump forming in my throat.

Mai looked at him sideways, pursed her lips and averted her eyes to gaze at the moon. The wife followed Mai's gaze, her eyes lingering there for a moment, and then she said, "But the good thing is we are coming back tomorrow, to spend the day here, then go back in the evening to sleep, and come back again Thursday, do the same thing, until the weekend." She concluded her announcement with a smile like a crescent moon, a watermelon slice of a smile, but her eyes looked troubled, guilty even. I wanted them to look guilty.

"Going to town tonight, coming back tomorrow, going back again and again, doesn't your car eat your money that way?" asked Mai with a splintered voice.

"It's not like we are driving to Bulawayo," the wife said. "Just twenty kilometres, that's all."

Ranga, now looking at his watch, said, "We still have a few minutes, to talk some more. Ask us about anything. Then, maybe, we can leave in twenty minutes." He looked at Mai, who didn't react. "How does that sound, mother? That's better than not staying a bit longer, right?"

"Iwe!" said the wife. "Sh-h-h-h!"

Ranga shrugged. Mai forced a smile and leaned forward, chewing her lower lip. I did the same and leaned against the wall.

They sat down.

African Roar

There was a moment of silence. We sat there as if we didn't know what to do next. I was still trying to understand Ranga's plans. Not only that. I had to begin working on deciding whether I would ever understand my brother ever again. More troubling was the fact that I still didn't know if he was being serious. When Mai broke the silence and commented about how bright the moon was, I sighed, sat back and prepared to hear what they wanted to talk about before taking off.

Ranga asked me about the women he had liked as a boy, and the wife had no idea what he was talking about. Poor woman, maybe she thought he was talking about some relatives, which could explain why she sat there grinning. I just looked at her, thinking, don't worry, his childhood sweethearts are all dead.

When her turn to talk came, Noma told us, again, that she was born in Gwanda, but she had grown up in Gweru, which explained why her Karanga was good. She had left the country in 2000 to finish school in America, where she met my brother, whom she found still reading his Shakespeare there. I liked how she reduced his advanced studies to the act of reading one man; I even laughed briefly. She said she worked for the State of California.

"That must pay a lot of money, Noma," I said, beginning to respect her. A woman who knew how to work for herself was my friend. As a former teacher myself, I understood these things. "Lots of money, I bet," I said.

"No, Tete, they pay peanuts," she said.

"It sure can't be as bad as things are here," I said.

"On that, I can't argue with you."

She had managed to help her parents move to America too. With the parents living there, Ranga found it easier to pay his bride price. The marriage took place in a small black church in Vallejo, Baptist... something. The name really didn't matter, as long as I knew that they were properly married. It would have been nice if they had cared to invite us, to bring us there like she had brought her parents. I looked at my brother's face to see signs of shame, thinking maybe he would feel bad about what he had not done, but all I saw was a silly grin. When our eyes met, he said, "Her parents were reasonable. I paid only $5000 for everything. They told me that they were fellow refugees in a strange land and they understood that we were all suffering together."

What did we know? Mai and I had not been told a word of this by anyone. No letter about the marriage, nor even a message given to someone visiting the country. Through rumours we had heard that he lived with a woman and we had even thought she was white, and mother had started to tell the villagers about her white daughter-in-law, until someone told us that no, she was black too. Black American woman? No, they said, real African woman from here too, and Mai and I had said, *hezvo-o*, he had found one over there? Now it made sense that she thought America was "back home". Who wouldn't if her parents lived in America too?

I looked at her as she winked at my brother, maybe trying to stop him from saying too much. But she seemed like a good wife. And I was beginning to like everything she was telling us. Soon it would be our turn to tell them how things had been for us.

Ranga looked at his watch again and said, "It's that time folks."

So now we were folks? I didn't want to start anything, so I just listened, like the good sister I was, but I had to know what he was talking about. "Time for what?" I asked.

"You know, like we said before," he said, showing me his wrist watch.

"You are going back already?" Mai asked.

Ranga said, "Just to sleep. We'll come back tomorrow, as Noma already said." He stood up, stretched and started walking to the car. The wife rose too, but lingered on the same spot like she wanted to embrace us.

I was waiting to see if they were just going to get in that car and drive off. At least they should sit for another two hours to give us a chance to talk about ourselves too. But Ranga got into the car and started it.

As the car growled, Mai walked to the driver's side and said, "So if you are going back to your overseas on Saturday we will continue to sleep outside then?"

"Why do you think so, mother?" he asked, dropping his shoulders like he had always done as a boy.

"What am I supposed to say? You were gone for ten years, and my heart tells me once you go back that it will be another ten before I see you again; then when you think of coming back to finish the house, there will be no one to sleep in it." She paused to allow the braying of a nearby donkey to cease, and then said, "You know people die these days and some of us are not getting any younger."

"Why would you say that, mother?" asked the wife, walking up to stand closer to Mai.

"You are the one who drove around looking at all the graves. People die. It's by the grace of Mwari Wedenga that you found us alive. But once you leave, there is no telling that you will not be driving to see our graves when you come back."

"I will pay someone to finish the house before we leave," Ranga said, loudly. Then lowering his voice, he added, "No one is going to die, and we will not spend another ten years in America before we come to visit again."

"It has happened before, it can happen again," Mai said. "For a long time I thought you were dead, you know. Why do you do such things to your mothers?"

"I was working and going to school. I wanted to make sure that you had something to eat and somewhere to sleep."

We all turned to look at the house.

Mother said, "We thank you for the house. What mother wouldn't be proud?" The calmness of her voice as she pointed at the house that was not a house surprised me, but I knew she was about to explode with anger.

The wife said, "We're very sorry, mother." Then to her husband, with a raised voice, she said, "Maybe we should just sleep with the others here."

"We are not like 'the others'," Ranga snapped, then looked around as if to make sure we were not looking and not hearing him. He lowered his voice and said, "Unlike 'the others', we have laptops and phones to charge."

Somehow I still thought he was joking; he had to be. Some sick boyish joke; otherwise, I would never learn to understand this. Apparently, judging by the volume of his voice, he was not joking. He said, "Do you get it? Phones, laptops-."

"Ranga, don't be ridiculous!" Noma said, shaking her head in a way that sent the braids flying. "Who cares about the stupid laptop and phone?"

"You of all people should know what I'm talking about. Look at this place," he said, then threw his hands on his lap when he saw that she was still shaking her head. "You know we already booked that place."

"So?" said the wife, clicking her tongue.

My lips were shaking with a smile that felt really good. The $5000 bride price had gone to her parents for a good reason. I moved closer to her. The look on Ranga's face was priceless. My sister-in-law said, "You should be ashamed of yourself acting like... acting the way you are right now."

But Ranga shifted in the car seat. I thought he was going to come out, but he sat back and said, "Why are you being such a pain all of a sudden?" His voice was shaking. "I try to seek comfort for you and all you do is nag, always trying to have things your way? You think we are in-." But he didn't finish. In fact, he lowered his eyes and looked at his hands instead.

"What did you say?" the wife spoke, leaning forward to the car window. "Because if you said something, say it again!" She swung and looked at me, but her ear was still tilted to my brother.

Ranga hesitated. But he took one look at Mai, then at me, and I could see him stiffen, like the man of the house. "You can't have it both ways, trying to run things there, and trying to run them here too. We are home now — ekhaya."

So now he was Ndebele too? I moved closer to hear this. And the wife said, "I don't just try, I do what I have to do: otherwise who else would do what needs to be done?"

There was a moment of silence that seemed to confuse both the wife and the husband. Mai had turned away and I could not tell if she was still chewing her lips. I wasn't going to pretend I had heard a word of what my brother's wife had just said. I didn't want to get involved.

"I'm going to that hotel with or without you," Ranga said in a voice meant to be authoritative, but even I could tell that no one was affected by it seriousness, certainly not this sister-in-law of mine.

Ranga slammed the door closed and said, "Ciao."

"Fine then. Go!" the wife said, her voice trying to beat the loudness of the enraged engine. Then she began to march away from the car, but she stopped, turned, and shuffled back to the car. She leaned forward and said, "I'll sleep here with the others." She threw her arms in the air and marched back to where we stood.

Ranga made as if he was about to get out of the car to follow her, but sunk back into the seat. He grabbed the steering wheel tightly with both hands and stiffened. After a while he rolled down the window and stuck his head to look at us like a mad person.

"She said you can go," I shouted.

He turned the car off and yelled at the wife, "You've gotta be kidding me! Are you coming or what?"

"It was your idea to keep sending the money through Fati, even though you knew he could not be trusted. Now does this look like a house of a mother who has a son in the

117

Diaspora? Look at it! Come closer and look! Do you even have eyes?"

"Don't use those kinds of words to each other," said Mai, as she retreated towards her mat. Her voice was subdued, like she was done talking for the night.

"Let them sort themselves out mother; you can't get in their things," I said.

My brother pulled the keys out, leaned back, and looked at the roof of the car.

"Go, my children, go to sleep in town," Mai said. "My heart wouldn't be happy to see you sleep with us here. This is not a place for people to sleep in."

Brother started the car again and it growled impatiently.

"You better go because you are making noise," said the wife.

"Why do you care? You who didn't want to come here in the first place?"

"Don't start Mr. I-am-afraid-of-germs-out-there. If it was up to you someone would have been sent here to pick up mother and Tete."

"To go where?" I asked, edging closer to the car. "Some of us love free rides."

"Tete, if I had let him, right now you would be with us at the hotel in Zvishavane; then at the end of the week he would have put you on the bus to come back here."

"You should have let him do that," said mother. "That's what good wives do. Didn't you say he paid roora for you there in overseas?"

The wife opened her mouth, but nothing came out. It was clear she had least expected this one from Mai. And for some reason, Mai's voice had sounded serious, like she was upset with the wife and was suddenly on her son's side. That wouldn't be fair, so I had to say something.

"What are you talking about mother?" I asked, following her to the mat. "I thought you wanted him to come see the house. Besides, why are you asking her about roora? It's not like he could just choose not to pay it. You raised him well."

"Let them go to town. It's not good for people to see a car parked where there is no real house," she said, lying down.

"Mother, you are not making sense," I said, joining her on the mat, but I didn't lie down. "Don't confuse people."

"People will talk, you know they will," she said, and she was both right and wrong.

I had to tell her that, speaking loudly enough for my brother to hear. "You talk about people talking. They have been talking for ten years, and they are talking right now. Maybe they are in the bushes looking and listening. But who cares about them? That's why they are called people."

The wife joined us on the mat. She sighed, and then tilted her head. Her massive braids fell to one side, like they had a mind of their own.

"Mother, no one is going back to town," she said. "We'll all sleep here, then work to get this house finished before we leave."

"The house doesn't matter," Mai said. "It's the years. Ten years is not a joke, people."

"Exactly what I told your son when I met him and he told me his story."

"And you still married him?" I asked, laughing.

She gave me one of her confused looks, with her cheeks dropping like she was about to cry.

"I'm just joking. My brother is a good man," I said.

The car started and lurched forward. We all looked at it as it took off.

"Is he leaving you?" Mai said. "That's not the son I raised."

"He can do what he wants; he is a grown man."

"Not if he leaves like this," I said, standing up. "He's making me angry."

He drove past the old donkey pen, then circled the empty goat pen, and slowed down.

A Return to Moonlight

"Maybe he is looking for a place to relieve himself," I said. "There is no toilet here."

He made the car roar, and then he drove faster, only to come to a complete stop. Maybe the dreams I had been having of him going mad were coming true. What was he doing, such a grown man, behaving like a donkey? If he was not careful he could drive into the ditch by the goat pen; I would laugh and laugh. That would teach him a lesson.

He made a u-turn and drove back slowly, stopped, reversed, then drove forward again. This time he drove past the Muzeze tree and parked at the edge of the compound, turned the lights off, and jumped out. But he lost his balance and fell flat on his stomach. When he shot up she started jumping around and punching the air as if he was doing some exercises. That's when we laughed, the wife and I. Very loud laughter — *chikuwe chaicho*.

"What happened?" Mai asked, suppressing her laughter.

"He fell *sedamba*," said the wife, still wailing with laughter.

"Oh," said Mai. "People fall all the time." She then broke into laughter too, but ended up just coughing, one of her coughs that could last long.

Ranga stood there looking at us, maybe wondering what was funny; and then he brushed dust off his knees and stomach. He fished his phone out and tried to turn it on, but the light didn't come on. "Dead and useless!" he shouted, and we laughed even louder.

He shook his head and made the phone find its way back into the pocket where it belonged. Then he came and sat on his childhood stool.

When our laughter and mother's coughing stopped, Ranga looked at the moon and said, "1987."

We ignored him; in fact, I thought he was talking to himself, or was reciting something, like back when he used to write things he called poems. But he raised his voice and said, "The year, 1987."

"What about it?" Noma asked. "Are you dreaming now?"

"The moon reminds me of the year."

"Ok… And?" she said.

"Ask Tendi. She knows how I used the moon back then," Ranga said.

"Do you know what he's talking about, Tete?"

"No idea," I said. "Why don't you tell her about the moon?"

"I used it for light," he said.

"Light?" Noma said.

"For my O-Level exams. That's how I studied for them, outside, in the light of the moon. On this very stool," my brother said, chuckling. He then looked at the moon and as we followed his gaze he said, "Don't you remember? Tendi? Mother?"

"Oh Lord," the wife said. "Now he is getting into one of his endless childhood stories. We might as well sit back, relax." She looked at me and nodded a warning. "This may take forever."

"Let him bring it on," I said as I lay on the mat.

I didn't know exactly what Ranga was talking about, or what I was supposed to remember, but then again, there were many things that I had taught myself to forget.

A Return to Moonlight

Emmanuel Sigauke, co-editor of *African Roar*, is a Zimbabwean writer based in Sacramento, California where he teaches English and Creative Writing at Cosumnes River College. He has published poetry and fiction in various magazines. He co-edits the following print and online journals: *Cosumnes River Journal, Tule Review*, and *Munyori Literary Journal*. He has published a poetry collection entitled *Forever Let Me Go*, and some of his poems appeared in *State of the Nation: Contemporary Zimbabwean Poetry*. He is working on a collection of his short stories.

African Roar

Truth Floats

Nana Awere Damoah

The spider worked tirelessly, spinning her web in the corner of the cubicle. It was a huge web with intricate designs. The spider hummed as she worked, tired but hopeful, hopeful that good work yielded great dividends. Didn't the elders say that the one who should enjoy the meal is the one who laboured?

The fly was enjoying his flight through the nice ambience in the room. The day's peregrinations had been fruitful. He had travelled far and wide, and enjoyed various substrates. He was in high spirits and had already started looking forward to a good night's sleep. The wind was his friend, the air was his companion, and he knew no enemies. It has been said many times by the sages that our most vulnerable times are the immediate moments after victories or great successes. It can be added that after a good meal, one can also be vulnerable, and that was the state the fly was in.

It was with such warm thoughts and with such abandon that the fly flew directly into the spider's web. The fly's house was just around the corner and here he was stuck in the trap of the dreadful, wicked spider. The fly struggled to get out of the entanglement, silently praying that the spider was asleep. His prayer went unanswered.

The spider spied the fly, and with a contented smile crawled towards her victim. It is only the tongue that can interpret a palatable meal, thought the spider as she moved towards the fly. The fly struggled to go free, but fate and time were not on his side, as the spider moved towards him for the kill, with the fly struggling, struggling, and struggling, but in vain...

Blowing over the quiet ambience of the University campus, the cold harmattan winds did nothing to counter the heat in the packed Room 61M of Nyaniba Hall. Akoto woke up with a start, sweating as if he had been in a struggle. He felt hotness on his skin, and got up to sit on his bed. His room-mate slept on, snoring like a scooter whose exhaust pipe had burst. Kweku M. Ananse was his name and he was the most carefree person Akoto had ever seen. So full of life and ideas.

Kweku, the Ananse. The only son of his father. The senior Ananse, whose first name Owawani became synonymous with slyness in his village of Hiawa. Story goes that after five daughters had been born to Owawani, his desire for a male heir became so intense he almost cursed the gods. So when Kweku was born, his father Owawani was over the moon.

Before Kweku's birth, the elders of the Ablade clan, Owawani's family, had come to his house at dawn. The delegation of four elders was led by Abusuapanyin (head of clan) Kwaw Abora, a cranky old man of indeterminate age, who was famous for his sharp tongue and for getting straight to the point.

After the customary serving of water and small talk – about the weather, the harvest, the chieftaincy disputes in the neighbouring villages – Owawani cleared his throat, a signal that he wanted to speak.

One of the elders, Mensu Kyekyeku, apart from the Abusuapanyin, acted as the linguist of the delegation and it was to him that Owawani addressed this statement.

"Kyekyeku, let Opanyin Abora know that here in my house all is well. The elders say that we may know yet we still ask, and that the matter from outside the house is usually sweeter than what is in the house. You have come, kindly let me know your mission."

Kyekyeku turned to Opanyin Abora and relayed the message to him.

"Opanyin, this is what your son Owawani is asking; he says we have come, so he is eager to know what brought us here at this early hour when he should be doing what real men do before their wives wake up to sweep." A murmur of laughter went round the gathered men.

Opanyin Abora called the meeting to order.

"Agoooo."

"Ameeee," the others responded.

"Agooo."

"Ameee."

"Anuanom, agooo."

"Ameee."

Opanyin Abora went straight to the core of their mission: the family had taken note that Owawani's wife Akosua Serwaa had been producing only girls. Investigations into her family had revealed that it wasn't unusual: most of her sisters had female offspring.

"Did the elders not say that when a woman makes a shield, it is stored in a man's room, and also that a woman may buy a shotgun but keeps it in the corner of a man's room? Owawani, we want you to take a second wife, so you can get a male heir. I am done."

That was two years before Kweku Ananse was born, and Owawani was glad that he was proved right by sticking to his only wife Akosua Serwaa, a moral victory for the man who otherwise considered morals the bread of cowards.

The hall clock, which was reputed to be as old as the University, chimed five times. The myth was that when the clock stopped chiming, the University would produce the premier first class student in Physics. And the story went that to prevent this, the Physics department set a tithe of its budget each year aside to ensure the clock was always in good shape. Akoto didn't mind that story much; all he cared for was that the clock was as reliable to offer the correct time as his room-mate and friend, Kweku, was in being mischievous.

Akoto didn't remember the last time he had dreamt. Even if he did, he didn't remember the full plot when he woke up. Kweku was the dreamer; he had a tale to tell each morning. And you could be sure to hear another tale if he slept in the afternoon. Akoto teased him that his many dreams resulted directly from the sumptuous meals he ate each night, before he slept. That and the fertile ground for constructing mischief, the ground he called his brain. Kweku the smart guy, Kweku the mischief, Kweku the fox.

It was five thirty in the morning and try as he did, Akoto couldn't go back to sleep. The dream was simply interesting and he couldn't find anything useful to brood over in it. Spiders always weaved webs and that was not news at all.

"Massa, wake up, wake up", Akoto tried to rouse Kweku from his sleep.

The man slept like a puff adder that slept both day and night because it couldn't distinguish between the two.

"Kweku! It is time to get ready for lectures!" Akoto persisted.

"Hmm, hmmm, won't man get any peace in this world at all? What is it, eh, what koraa is the matter?"

"Time for bathing, lazy booonnnnneeessss!"

"Kai! And I haven't ironed too!"

With that, the Spiderman jumped from his bed. He was nicknamed the Spiderman because of his surname. As first, he wasn't too pleased with the alias, but after watching the movie Spiderman, he realized the character really epitomized what he, Kweku Ananse, could achieve: almost anything. To Kweku, the whole world was like a draught board and the smartest player could always win the game. The rules of the game were: the end justifies the means. It is only the squirrel that sang that things must be done in the right way. In the gospel according to Kweku Ananse, life was hard and the smart took it by force. His father had made it through life by being smart and the offspring of the snake could not be short. The elders had advised that one should not be happy when people remark that you were a chip of the old block, because your father might have been a questionable character. But Kweku loved it so. He was indeed the Spiderman.

At birth, Kweku's father had looked intently at his son, searching for any resemblance; he found one immediately – the head, and particularly the back of the head. Many had described the back of Owawani Ananse's head as resembling that of a yawning bird. Owawani's retort had always been that it housed a brain of immense capabilities, and that was the same level of intelligence Owawani prayed for his son, because though all heads may look alike, the ideas in them may differ!

Owawani had chosen his son's name, as soon as he was told his wife had gone into labour at the hospital. He would call him Kweku Ananse. Kweku because he was born on a Wednesday. Ananse was the family name, in the Akan language referring to the spider.

The eighth day after the birth of the little boy, the outdooring took place to name him, to give him an identity. It is believed that before the eighth day, a newly born child was still in a dilemma whether to stay on earth or go back to the land of the ancestors. After eight days, one was quite sure then the child would stay, and it is at that point that the child was given a name. Before then, it was called Hey, an ambiguous name.

Egya Ananse, as the father was known by all, was a happy man on that day. In Hiawa, the name of the parent almost vanished as soon as kids were added to the family. The mother of Mansa became Mansa Maame, and the father Mansa Papa. Now Owawani Ananse was called

Kweku Papa, a name he relished as if he had earned it on the battlefield. His chest heaved at the mere thought of that. He could now take his rightful place under the Nim tree where the men gathered to play draughts and discuss events after work, fortified with palm wine drunk from calabashes. He had shown that his waist was not just for dancing and production of girls – he now had a boy to prove that his loins had come of age.

Akoto was already in the bath-house when Kweku left the room. It was Tuesday, and they both met Ama Adoma at the Mecca bridge to escort her to lectures, hence the early rise.

Ama Adoma. The only one advantage his friend Akoto had over him. The prettiest girl he had ever seen in his fast life. Her neck was like ringed sausages, earning her the name Ama Konfe, the girl with the beautiful neck. When she smiled, her cheeks reformed into two dimples, which could hold two pebbles with ease. Her lips parted to reveal teeth set neatly by each other like footballers arranged in a defence wall before a free kick, sparkling white like fresh cotton buds against background savannah grass. Her walk was like that of a graceful Adowa dancer. The most beautiful lady on campus and she was Akoto's fiancée.

A rich, white sky laced with blue looked down on the earth that morning. It had rained the previous night and the streets were strewn with leaves and dead branches. The fragrance of earth, leaves, roses, and soil permeated the ambience.

The grass still held morning dew, forming cute little droplets on the surfaces of the leaves. There was no wind, no sunshine. It was all serene, peaceful.

Adoma's face matched the spirit of the morning. As usual, it was radiant with joy. She sang as she descended the stairs of Yaa Asantewaa Hall, a song she had been singing from the bathroom.

Truths Floats

When peace like a river,
Attended my way.
When sorrows like sweet billows roll.

She went through the great doors opposite the P-Lodge and into the street. Her heart was full of song and she was at peace. It felt good to be alive!

Whatever my lot,
Thou hast taught me to say.
It is well, it is well,
With my soul.

Others on their way to lectures passed her. Some waved and hurried on. She preferred to pass through Nkrumah Hall. The path under the trees was part of her route. As she went down the hilly plain towards the roundabout, Adwoa bypassed her. Her room-mate was always in a hurry. Adoma looked at her wrist watch, and realised she had enough time to move on at her normal pace.

It is well, it is well,
With my soul, with my soul.
It is well, it is well,
With my soul.

Kweku and Akoto were both in their final year at the University College of Amenfi, and had a final semester to go. Kweku was as evasive about his hometown as he was about the secondary school he attended; he didn't divulge much. When pushed to the wall to share a bit about himself, Kweku was known to say to his questioners that if you searched too deeply under the eyes of a corpse, you were certain to see a ghost. But his cunning and cleverness you couldn't take away from him. Sometimes, Akoto wondered whether his friend really sat for any examinations at all, before entering the University.

"Kweku, please hurry up. We are running late."

"Ho ho, you and your pushing with respect to Adoma, why? Is she a time-bomb? Will she explode if we don't get to her on time?"

"Charlie, you can play with your fiancée when you get one. As for me, I won't let any other person take away my girl with TLC – tender loving care. I will guard her like an Iraqi government minister!"

"Even the Queen of England is not treated like your Adoma. Anyway, I am ready. Let me not be the reason for any break-ups. But remember, there is bound to be a knot in any long string."

On their way to the Mecca Bridge Hall, Akoto thought of what Kweku had said. Akoto's mum lived in the United Kingdom and thus he travelled abroad on most vacations. His visa had already been obtained and he was due to travel right after his final examinations. He wanted to spend a couple of years, slave away there and come back to Ghana to wed his queen. Even the vulture which is not edible nursed its eggs in the branches of a high tree, because man is hard to trust and eggs are delicacies!

Adoma was near the Mecca bridge now. A smile broke over her pretty face when she saw Akoto, with his faithful friend Kweku by his side. She linked her arms with his, and they continued to the lecture area.

Akoto didn't want to keep Adoma waiting too long after school before marriage and didn't want to be too far away from her. A glance at Adoma by his side reinforced his resolve to marry her in the shortest possible time.

"What a beauty", thought Kweku, as he also stole a glance at Adoma as they walked to the lecture hall. His plans were still under construction within his mind. Wasn't it said that young people kept their money in the pocket of their parents?

Kweku had no problem with getting girlfriends; the problem was in retaining them. Kweku once went out with a girl called Akua Kyeiwaa. Kyeiwaa used to tell everyone – who cared to listen – that in her relationship with Kweku, she had to do all the work in maintaining and sustaining their relationship, likening it to a bone running after a dog.

But Adoma was special, and he was beginning to like her a lot. A tooth lost its respect and place in an aching jaw and a gold nugget could never sparkle besides charcoal. Adoma was fit for him, Kweku, and have her he would. Only in the community of pregnant women does an over-matured coconut dropped on its own accord, and Kweku was neither a pregnant woman nor was he living in such a community. He was the smartest man on campus and he would certainly pluck this ripe coconut – Adoma.

Kweku knew he would have to call on all his skills and fertile schemes, and he was prepared for it. He didn't mind the fact that this could bring a rift between him and Akoto, because however kind a man was, he would not give his wife as a gift to his friend. He would bide his time and strike at the right time, for it was with patience that the experienced hunter killed an elephant. Kweku felt that he was entitled to Adoma, on the same level as Akoto. Wasn't he the go-between for the two lovebirds in the early days of their relationship and even now? Didn't he help Akoto win Adoma? Indeed, a bedfellow in sowing the seed should be a part in the harvest, he reasoned. He didn't mind what people would say when he succeeded. Ethics, friendship, betrayal of trust - all stupid impediments! It was only the coward who was scared by the scarecrow, and Kweku believed that he wasn't a coward at all – no scheme was out of his bounds.

One day Adoma visited their room. Akoto wasn't in the room; he had a project proposal to defend. Adoma sat on Akoto's bed as she sipped the Coca Cola Kweku bought for her from the hall canteen.

"So how are studies, Adoma?" Kweku asked.

"Hmm, not too bad oo. I am managing, but sometimes I get too stressed out with Economics. It is getting better though."

"OK, good. Tell me, Adoma, how are you going to sustain the love you have for Akoto when he travels? I understand long-distance relationships are difficult to maintain."

"Ah Kweku! When you love someone, distance doesn't matter oo, only love does."

"Yoo, my mouth is a bucket! Me, I am only asking. But when you are a child and you see the eyes of a crab, you say they are sticks."

Kweku did his best to tell tales about Adoma to Akoto, slipping in little innuendoes about her escapades. Akoto kept his cool about Adoma, insisting that if the eye hadn't seen it, it was not dirty. As long as he hadn't heard from two or three witnesses, he would continue to trust his queen.

Akoto had to travel abroad after his final examinations in July. On the departure day, Kweku, Adoma and Akoto travelled together to Accra for his flight. The parting was emotional; it was difficult for both Akoto and Adoma, and Kweku joined in their tears. Kweku played the part of a sympathetic friend who had to weep just because he was part of the funeral procession, but in his heart, he rejoiced at the way fate was conniving with his intentions. The owner of the house was going away, and was also leaving the meat in the care of the cat, Kweku! Kweku intended to feast on that meat; after all, he was no bodyguard who only protected a property without exploiting it.

When the final boarding call was made, Adoma rushed into Akoto's arms yet again. A flood of tears overflowed the banks of Adoma's eyes, and Akoto had to struggle not to join her. He smiled wryly when he remembered the saying that a man was not supposed to cry. Such difficult advice to follow when your loved one was weeping on your shoulders with emotions strong enough to even stir the chords of an Ibo man's heart!

Since Adoma was not staying in the city, didn't have access to the Internet and also couldn't get letters through regular mail, Akoto decided that he would be writing frequently through Kweku.

"Akoto, my friend", Kweku promised, "I will do my best to ensure that communication between the two of you is not broken. After all, the mushroom and the hill have not thanks between them. They are one and the same. What is yours is mine to maintain for your sake."

"Me d'ase, Kweku. You have been such a good friend, and my heart is light knowing you are here for me."

Six months had passed since Akoto left, and Adoma was doing her National Service in Wasa Asikuma. For four months, she had not heard from Akoto at all. Not even a letter. Kweku Ananse called her at the Post office weekly and always said Akoto was yet to send a single letter down for her. She had received two or so letters in the initial months following his departure and then, nothing.

After school each day, she took a walk along the road towards Ankonsia, alone with her thoughts. One day she took the path that went towards Moseaso, by the peaceful flowing waters of the Ankobra that lovingly washed the rocks in an intricate, ancient ritual, undisturbed by the passage of time. She walked alone as usual, in silence, deep in thought, oblivious that it was getting dark, as the villagers returned from their farms, and waved at her. She didn't notice. She only thought of Akoto. Indeed, the elders were right when they said the mouth that was used to source a loan was not the same one used to pay it. Akoto had promised her heaven, and sworn to keep her in perpetual touch. Adoma was disappointed and was becoming increasingly disillusioned with Akoto. Her only consolation and forte of strength in the hard times had been Kweku Ananse.

Kweku's plan was working to perfection. Parcels were made to facilitate easy recovery. And he made sure that with each visit and call to Adoma, his hidden message was easily deciphered. Initially, he had forwarded Akoto's letter to Adoma, to give her the impression that if Akoto should write, Ananse would promptly deliver the letters. He had even travelled the whole night to Asikuma, arriving at dawn, just to prove the point that he (Kweku) treated Akoto's letters with urgency.

But when two bosom friends vie for same lady, they have chosen a common road to be each other's enemy. Kweku was determined to win this war. Kweku was the linguist in this affair, the middle man in this relationship. Did the elders not say that only the linguist could blow the chief's ivory horn to sing his highnesses eulogy? Kweku had decided to blow the horn and produce a tune favourable to him. He held on to subsequent letters from Akoto to Adoma and also kept those from Adoma to Akoto. His weekly calls and occasional visits to Wasa increased.

"Kweku, this is your friend, what sort of life is this? Eh, how can he treat me this way?" Adoma asked Kweku one afternoon in Asikuma.

It was in August, about a year following Akoto's departure and many months since Adoma heard from him.

"Adoma, the head is not a coconut that you can open to see what is inside it. Though he is my friend, I cannot explain all his actions," Kweku said, looking at the beautiful girl before him. Ah, such a beauty, Kweku said to himself the umpteenth time. How true it was that only a toothless cat would not lick his lips when a mouse was playing near his nose. Kweku was enjoying the game he was playing with this beautiful mouse and his lips were getting even worn out from all the licking!

"But Kweku, why? I have always been a faithful partner to your friend. And I have not given him any cause for him to treat me like this!"

"You can understand some men. You usually don't know the worth of someone until she leaves you. In school, we had a prayer we prayed in the dining hall: some want but they don't get; some get what they don't want..."

"But we want and we get so we thank thee oh Lord!" Adoma finished, and they laughed together.

Adoma's tone turned serious: "Kweku, what do you mean by that?"

"Oh, no, nothing serious. Except that, to the blind, the antics of the monkey and his gesticulations would never be enough to excite. But the monkey would seriously entertain the discerning with the same dance!"

Kweku left that evening for Accra (that day he left earlier than usual because he said his bank was organising a week long course for all its banking staff – Kweku was the Human Resources officer). After his departure, Adoma chewed long and hard on his words. Was Kweku telling her that she was blind and not seeing how good he, Kweku, had been to her in those trying times? Kweku was good-looking and had been good, too good, to her. A bird in hand was worth two in the bush, and there was no use waiting for those two in the bush, especially when they still had wings to fly! Who knew what Akoto was doing in the United Kingdom?

"But Adoma, your love for Akoto has not evaporated, has it?" her inner voice debated with her.

"I know, I still love him. He is my first love, and it is very difficult to get over him. In fact, I am confused."

The inner voice didn't give up its advocacy for Kweku.

"See, there is no one who has been faithful to you in these trying times than Kweku. Just consider how he comes regularly all the way to this village to see you. How many letters have you not written to Akoto? Tell me, how many of them has he replied? Tell me! When you asked Kweku to ask Akoto about the way forward, wasn't Akoto evasive?"

"Well, yes, that is what Kweku told me. I really don't know what to do!"

Meanwhile, Akoto was surprised Adoma hadn't written to him after the very first letter, and that was in the first month he arrived. Thoughts of her filled his every waking minute and he went to sleep each night reminiscing about their days together. Beautiful, lovely, sweet Adoma. He was on track with his promise to return in a year and a half, and he was slaving away, doing odd jobs to accumulate funds. Anytime he bent down to clean the hospital floor, each time he was abused by some of his colleagues at the construction site where he worked on weekends, on the occasions he missed the bus and had to walk in the cold weather because he had to rush from lectures to the security job where he worked thrice a week on night shift, he thought about Adoma. He had bought most of the items needed for both the customary rites (engagement) and the wedding. He had also prepared his costume for the two ceremonies. There was so much he needed to discuss with Adoma at that point – and so much to plan. But her silence puzzled him.

The only letters he received from Ghana were from his buddy Kweku Ananse, and they did not convey good news. In one instance, Kweku reported that Adoma was the secret girlfriend of the chief of Wasa Asikuma. Kweku said after several chats with her to put a stop to the immoral affair, she still persisted. To Akoto's query why Adoma wasn't writing to him, Kweku asked him how someone who is busily enjoying a sumptuous meal would have time to talk. Yet Akoto didn't lose hope and continued to write, care of Ananse his trusted friend.

Kweku the banker was seriously enjoying the game, and the web he was spinning around Adoma and Akoto. He walked into his dedicated cabinet where he kept the letters of the two lovebirds. The cabinet was divided into two, with labels: Adoma and Akoto.

"Stupid Akoto! Such a fool" he laughed. "A foolish man in a pensive mood is making no judicious plan, he is a still a buffoon," Kweku said aloud, falling down on the floor in uncontrollable hilarity.

When Kweku proposed to Adoma in October, Adoma's patience had waned and she was angry as well. Akoto had treated her shabbily, and she wanted to pay him back!

"Adoma, hold on, wait for your love; you know Akoto will not disappoint you, something must be wrong!" That inner voice again.

"No!" This time her mind took over. She willed for her heart to see reason with her mind. "I can't wait forever for him. Life is too short to be wasted on someone who takes his loved one for granted."

The tussle between that voice which sided with her heart and her mind went on for weeks. She became stressed with this inner struggle. It showed in her blank face, devoid of that buoyant expression her pupils and colleagues alike loved so much.

Two years went by and still no news of Akoto reached her. Adoma finally gave in to the incessant pressure from Kweku. The wedding at the Holy Tabernacle of the Lord, the latest charismatic church in town, was planned and executed in record time. Kweku convinced Adoma that, knowing her family's preference for Akoto, it was not prudent to involve them. And in any case, before anyone took the message to them in Dunkwa-on-Offin, the wedding would have been over, and the deal sealed. With the certificate of notice from the local authorities, they approached the church and had the quiet wedding.

Kweku had won the target of two years and he felt so satisfied. In a little over a month, he was ready to move on to his new target. He had trapped the crab and not the water in it. The water could flow away for all he cared!

In December, three years after Akoto had travelled and more than a year later than he had promised to come back, he returned to Ghana. He had used his time abroad to study part-time for his law degree. He was so excited on his flight back home. He had not been faithful to his promise, but he was sure Adoma would understand. Especially when he had written to both Adoma herself and Kweku – so he could add his voice to his plea – explaining his delay. Now, he was going to marry the love of his youth. Not hearing from Adoma all these years heightened his excitement further.

On his arrival, he went straight to Kweku's home and that was where he came crushing down to earth! His love, the object of his attention, the reason for his almost slave-like toil in a foreign land, the lady of his heart had married in his absence! And to the one person he trusted above all, save God!

He rushed from Kweku's house, went straight back home, and wept. Between his bouts of sobbing, he spoke to his empty room.

"Ah Kweku! Ah ah ah! If anyone would do this to me, it shouldn't have been you! Why did you have to prove our elders right that the ant that will bite you is in your own cloth, eh?"

He couldn't forget the smile of victory on Kweku's face as he left his friend's house. Finally, it was this image of his smiling friend that stopped his copious tears. Did the elders not say that one could not weep and meditate at the same time? Akoto decided to do all he could to wipe away that grin, nay smirk, from the face of the scoundrel. He decided to win back his love. Kweku had eaten his yam and Akoto was determined to let him choke on it. His father's words came to him: that if a snake came out a hole and invited you to dip your hand into it, there was nothing to be afraid of because the danger in that hole was already out. Kweku's trickery and strategy were already out and Akoto knew he could beat him at his own game.

The next day, he went to the school where Adoma was teaching. She had been transferred to Accra following her marriage. The reunion between the two was frosty at first.

At break time, Akoto was able to pull her away from her class to a quiet restaurant.

"Adoma, why? Why didn't you wait for me? Why?" Akoto was holding back tears.

"Eh, please hold on. See the black pot calling the kettle black! I should rather be asking you why you disappointed me so. Why you did not get in touch with me for so long? Why you did not reply my letters? Why you did not bother to write to me? Did you think for once that I am a human being, a woman with feelings?" Adoma let down the dam that held all her hurts, mixed with regrets.

"Are you telling me you never received the many letters I sent to you through Kweku? Even though you had written to me only once? Even when I was informed you were not being faithful to me!"

"Whaaat!! Me being unfaithful to you? You wrote to me through Kweku?"

"Yes, Adoma. I have always written, sharing all my experiences, and also explaining why I had to spend more time to complete my law studies. And I even wrote the latest last month, informing you I was coming back in December. Did you not receive that too?"

"Oh, Jesus!" That was all Adoma could say. She broke down and wept.

It became obvious to both of them that Kweku had played them apart, to his benefit.

"Adoma, I still love you and you know that. I know you still love me, and that would not change."

"Akoto, I do know you love me and I still do love you, but I am married to your friend, that cheat!"

They affirmed their love to each other and pledged to find a way to pay Kweku back in his own coin.

When Adoma told Akoto later that the customary rites were not even performed, Akoto knew he had Kweku by the scruff! Legally, the notice for marriage from the local authorities was valid only on the basis that customary marriage had been done. And also, the pastor of the church where the wedding was held had not been licensed by the municipal authority to perform marriages! Therefore, the marriage between Adoma and Kweku was null and void! The fact that Akoto was a lawyer played no small part in the investigations! Indeed, knowledge of the law had triumphed over trickery!

Trouble, it is said, is like a storm: it doesn't rain; it pours. Just about the same time that Kweku's marriage to Adoma was annulled, an audit at the Accra International Bank, where Kweku worked, revealed a serious scandal which Kweku was involved in.

But it is dangerous to underestimate a cunning man such as Kweku Ananse, son of Owawani Ananse, for a man that builds himself a house of lies usually provides himself with a large window through which to escape when he is in trouble. Before the police could lay their hands on Ananse, he bolted. He lived by the adage of the jungle that it was better to escape with shots and injury, than to be captured for the fire. And Kweku was in no mood for the prison.

The wedding of Adoma and Akoto was held in grand style at the Holy Ghost Cathedral, with the heads of the Orthodox churches in attendance. As for Kweku, Adoma and Akoto thought he had his due recompense. Why should the chicken weep and fast in sympathy for a hawk which is imprisoned? In their joy, they had no tears for Ananse, no. Adoma and Akoto can be seen on the streets of Accra, living happily!

Truths Floats

Nana Awere Damoah is a Ghanaian Chemical Engineer and British Council Chevening alumnus, educated in Ghana and the UK, and author of *Excursions in My Mind* and *Through the Gates of Thought*. He started writing when he was 17 and has had a number of his short stories published in the Ghanaian weeklies *The Mirror* and *The Spectator*. In 1997, he won the first prize in the Step Magazine National Story Writing Competition. Nana works with Unilever Ghana.

African Roar

Tamale Blues

Ayesha Harruna Attah

Of all the places she could be right now, this was the last she'd be caught dead in. A rickety old bus, sitting next to a hen peeking out of a basket. The State Insurance Bus rattled over a speed bump, making the hen squawk, its head darting in and out of the basket. Nana glared at her uncle who was unperturbed by the commotion, though sweat had gathered on his pink T-shirt, dyeing it red. She sat in the middle seat, which had been lifted five times already for someone to get out to pee, for someone to vomit, for someone's child to poop. She strained her head and watched the sky shade from indigo to pitch black by the time they reached Tamale. As the bus pulled into the station, hawkers flocked to its sides. Her uncle asked if she wanted anything. She shook her head. What she wanted, he couldn't provide her with now. All she wanted was for this useless vacation to be over, her body back in Accra, tucked in her bed, far away from squawking fowl and passengers who couldn't hold their bladders.

Only a week ago, she'd stood in front of the Accra International School, her excitement mounting at the prospect of a long holiday. She had hugged her friends, jumped into her mother's air-conditioned Toyota and made small talk with Mr. T. It had been a wonderful day, she remembered.

As she'd stared into the cars rolling by with sweating kids in brown and beige uniforms and others in the blue and white striped uniforms of AIS, a billboard advertising a Ghana Airways flight caught her attention. Her parents hadn't told her what her vacation plans would be yet, but she was sure they'd be sending her to Uncle Rodney in London. She had smiled at the thought of walking up and down Oxford Street with her cousins, shopping bags bursting with new clothes and shoes.

This was the moment she kept replaying to herself all through her bus ride to Tamale: how her mother had paid Mr. T and called her into the family room. How her mother had wiped sweat from her face with a small towel and turned on the TV.

"Hello, sweetie," her mother had said, her voice laced with sweetness.

"Hi, mummy," Nana said and kissed her mother's cheeks. She'd do anything now to take away the kiss.

"I met Mrs. Alhassan on my walk this morning. You know how she can talk when she catches you. She was going on about her family draining her…"

"Poor you." Nana was bored by all the inane details of her mother's walk and so picked up the remote control to find something to do with her hands.

"She said she just got back from Tamale."

"Oh, yeah?"

"So it gave me an idea. I told your father we should let you visit his mother there." Nana's thumb hovered over the up arrow on the remote control. That was all she could see: numbers, arrows, numbers and arrows merging into each other. Tamale?

"When?"

"Uncle Osman is going back on Monday so you can ride along with him."

"But, mummy… I was going to ask if I could go to Uncle Rodney's. Do I have any say in this?"

"You do, but you've never been to see the family in the north. When you're done with your A-levels, you may end up in England or America for school, but you should know

145

more about your own country first. You'll thank us later."
Her mother reached forward and pressed Nana's brow.
Nana frowned, stuck out her lower lip and pulled her head
back.

"How long am I going to be there? Is Mr. T. driving me?"

"Are you listening? I said your uncle is taking you."

"In his car?" Nana pushed her eyes open as widely as she
could, hoping this would make the answer yes.

"No, on an STC bus." Her mother untied and retied her
ponytail.

"You mean I'm going to sit in a public bus for 10 hours?"

"Nana, stop being melodramatic. I heard some of the STC
buses have air-conditioning."

Air-conditioning her foot, Nana thought, now lying on a
mattress covered with a pink cotton-polyester blend sheet.
It was her grandmother's bed, but now her grandmother's
round form was splayed on a green raffia mat imprinted
with the image of a mosque. She made out the outline of
two others in the dark. When she'd arrived at the
compound house with Uncle Osman, all the children had
rushed out to meet her, screaming in Dagbani. She'd stood
there, like a log. She'd smiled, because it was the polite
thing to do, even though she hadn't felt like smiling. When
they'd spoken, words of welcome she was sure, she had
had no clue what to say to them. She spoke to her
grandmother in Twi, her mother's language. Now she
turned on her side, insomnia and heat keeping her eyes
open. They still hadn't told her when she'd be going back
to Accra.

When she woke up the next morning, she found herself
alone in the room. The mats her grandmother and the other
two had slept on were rolled up behind the door. Across
from the bed a dresser was piled with aluminium pans,
enamel cooking pots etched with flower prints, and plastic
cups, one of which was brimming with sugar. A trail of

black ants started from under the dresser and ended in the sugar. She shuddered. She hated ants.

A girl her age walked and introduced herself as Sadiya. She said she was Nana's father's uncle's daughter; in effect her aunt. She would take Nana around after she had taken a shower, to greet the family, she said, rolling her r's. She asked Nana how her parents were in Accra, which came out as 'Akarrra'. She had boiled some water for Nana's bath, she said, clasped her waist and waited for Nana to get up and follow her to the shower.

Two sets of steps led to two doors, both green at the bottom. Nana hung her towel and sponge on the nails behind the first door and headed for the other room. A heavy stench hit her as she entered, accompanied with a low intermittent buzzing. In the middle was a concrete ledge with a hole. There were brown stains around the hole. Nana couldn't believe such a place existed. She dashed out, trying not to throw up, the bluebottle flies' buzzing ringing in her ears. As she entered the shower, she wondered what she'd done for her parents to punish her.

Nana and Sadiya got back from greeting the large extended family in the afternoon, the sun still high in the sky. The mothers from the four chalets of the compound house were outside, sitting on low wooden stools. Some stirred stews; others pretended not to look at what the stirrers were doing.

"So, my dear, how was town?" asked one of the pretenders, beckoning Nana to her.

Nana shrugged and smiled. She did not understand a word. Sadiya translated.

"Why can't you speak the language?" the pretender gave up and spoke in English. She drew Nana closer and hugged her playfully. "You should learn."

"I will try." She was sure her response came off as tired and insincere, which it was, and she didn't care. She sat down and started to observe the making of communal dinner. A man stepped out of one of the chalets. He wore shorts, slung a towel around his neck and held a buta, which meant he was probably on his way to perform his ablution. Her father had one of those. When she was young, she thought it was a kettle for drinking tea, until he'd explained. The man asked her something in Dagbani. She returned a blank stare. The women laughed, but she didn't care. The man had awoken something that was slowly being killed in her. He was beautiful, tall and dark. Yes he was. His chest was sculpted, just perfectly. He could be a model, one pinned to their lockers of AIS girls. One AIS girls would swoon over for.

"Welcome my daughter. I will talk to you when I return from prayers." He ruffled the hair of one of the stirrers. She must have been his wife.

"Hello," said Nana, staring through the glass of her auntie Fati's communication centre, placed smack in front of the compound house. "Sister Mimi, it's Nana. Is mummy there?"

"Oh hello, Nana. I'm so happy you're calling. No, mummy has gone out. Daddy is here. Hold on." Nana could picture Mimi plastering her mouth to the mouthpiece. And she still hadn't learned not to shriek into the phone.

"Hello." Her father cleared his throat.

"Hi, Daddy. What's up?"

"Nana. How are you? Are you ready to leave yet?" The television roared in the background – BBC news or a boxing game – the only channels he did not snore through.

"I am," Nana said. She thought of the man with his slender body. She could see the chalet he'd come out of from the communication centre. He was the only interesting person around. "No, actually. I'm fine," she said. "Only thing is I cannot use the pit latrine. Who invented that thing? I got instantly constipated when I went in there." Nana's father laughed so loudly she had to move the phone away from her ear.

"I used that for seventeen years of my life. It's part of your learning experience."

"Well, it's horrible. Can't you build your own mother a WC?" She was sure she was stepping over the respect boundary. With her mother she could say anything. With her father there was always a limit.

"Hopefully next year I'll visit and work on those projects. The old lady's whole compound needs work. Anyway, let me not finish your money. Greet everyone for me." He always had something to go back to, Nana thought as she replaced the yellowed handset.

The model had not come back to talk to her as he'd said he would. He'd gone to pray and disappeared. She'd almost given up on him when two days later he walked into her grandmother's room. He knelt down and greeted Nana's grandmother, who sat on her green mat, her lips moving silently, her fingers beading her rosary. Her wrinkled head was wrapped in a light lemon-green silk scarf. The model said something to her grandmother, and then in English told Nana he was stealing her for a while. Nana jumped out of the armchair, a little too enthusiastically.

"So where are we going?" she asked when she'd closed her grandmother's door behind her. Her voice was too high, too eager.

"I thought I would take you around. I've seen that you're not too happy here. I think you'll like the evening market."

"There's a market behind my school," Nana said. She never went to the market. That was Mimi's job. The only connection she had was the loud market that crescendoed only when they were having an interesting lesson, and never when Mr. Ansah was droning on about factorials. They walked by a row of compound houses that stood like gigantic boxes, all marked with small wooden doors at the bottom of a wall: signs of pit latrines. Nana was strangely happy. None of the boys in her class showed an interest in her, so to have this man, who was clearly a good number of years older, notice her, was a wonderful feeling.

"I haven't asked what your name is," she said.

"Call me Rafik. Your aunties and grandmother would want you to call me uncle, but I really don't care." He took long strides in his striped sweat pants and navy blue t-shirt.

"OK, Rafik. Do you have any children?" She tried to think of questions to ask him, to keep him talking, engaged.

"Yes. Two of them. They've gone to visit their grandmother in Salaga."

They crossed a huge dirt road streaming with bicycles and motorcycles. Dusk was setting in, and the dust from the roads filled the sky. The sun looked brown rather than orange and the sellers began to light their paraffin lamps. On a high table, one seller had piled mounds of meat covered in powder, the same orange as the dirt road they had just crossed. The smell of peanuts and spices permeated the air. She tapped his arm to make him stop for her to buy some of the meat.

"I'll get it for you." She didn't have time to protest, he was already bargaining with the seller.

He led them to a long bench. She offered him some of her meat but he shook his head. "I hope I'm not being nosey," she said. "You speak really well, how come you decided to stay here, and not go to Accra or Kumasi to work?" She bit into a piece of meat and clenched her teeth in expectation of a dismissal, because after the words had come out, she realised how they sounded: educated, enlightened people need not stay in Tamale.

"Oh, it's a long story," he said. "But I like living in Tamale."

"I didn't mean…"

"I understand," he said. "Once, I also had dreams of moving to Accra. But life happens."

"What do you mean?"

"I got my wife pregnant and had to stay with her." He blinked, looked at her and tapped her wrist. "So, my dear one, what plans do you have for your life?"

After hearing that bit of information, she was not sure what to say, "I am almost done with school. I'm writing my A-levels next year."

"You are beautiful, you sound smart. Don't let any boy or anyone spoil your plans." He suddenly looked away. "You know, I grew up not too far away from here. In Lamashegu." He pointed towards the west, where the brown sun was descending lower and lower.

"What was it like?"

"A simple life. Times have changed. My father was a farmer, but he saved enough money for my brother and me to go through secondary school. He wanted us to go to university, but he did not have the money to cover that. He hoped I would get a scholarship. My younger brother is now in the University of Ghana, on a scholarship. I could be there right now..." He had been tapping her wrist the entire time. He cleared the phlegm from his throat and spat.

"I'm sorry," Nana said, a little put off, but more sorry than disgusted. What would sorry do for him? she wondered.

"My children make me happy and I feel good in my heart that I decided to stay with Hawa. But I'm stuck." He stopped, looked into her eyes. "You're a very beautiful girl, you know? Don't let any man destroy what you've got." Nana looked away, his gaze too intense for her, and wondered why he kept repeating that.

Nana didn't want to go back to the compound house, but after walking around the market asking what this was, Rafik explaining what that was, he said her grandmother would be worried. She went back into her grandmother's room, her hand concealing an ivory-coloured bracelet he'd bought her.

"Hello? Speak clearly I can't hear you."

"Hello, mummy, it's Nana."

"Sweetie! How are you? Are you ready to come home?" Her voice sounded distant and the line was crackly. She was probably in her bedroom watching a movie because her father had hijacked the family room TV.

"No, no. I'm getting an education remember?"

"Ei, what's with the 180?"

"It hasn't been as bad as I thought."

"Your father told me about your pit latrine woes."

"Yes! I finally used it yesterday. I thought I was going to explode. I held my nose and closed my eyes. Those flies. Ugh. And you know what was worse?"

"What could be worse than that?"

"This morning, I saw a guy carrying the wooden box that sits in the pit. Mummy, carrying it on his head. The box was full and spilling and he was carrying it on his head!"

"How disgusting."

"Have you used one before?"

"No. So, when do you want to come home?"

"Mummy, I'm not sure yet." She looked at Rafik's chalet. "Give my love to daddy. Bye."

Nana walked out of her grandmother's room. It was Friday and clearly everyone had gone to the mosque. She was surprised Sadiya hadn't awoken her as usual to take a shower. She walked out to fetch a cup of water.

She saw his slender frame, bent over. He turned to look at her.

"Wow! Are we the only ones around here?" Rafik asked.

"I don't know," Nana said. "I thought I was the only one here, but you're here..."

"I'm going to pray. Let's chat when I finish."

Nana tried not to think about the opportunity that was presenting itself. Her stomach was aflutter, but she didn't want to acknowledge it. She didn't go back into her grandmother's room. Instead, after washing her mouth, she sat on a stool facing Rafik's house. It was just the two of them in the huge compound. What would happen? What could happen? What if the feeling was not mutual? What if he thinks of me as a pretty little girl that needs to be shown her hometown but nothing more? The door whined open and he walked out in a brown sports jersey. He brought out a mat and spread it by Nana's stool.

"I should be sleeping now," he said. "I'm working late tonight."

"So go and sleep then. Don't mind me, I'll just go back inside to read."

"Oh no, don't worry. I'll be fine. I like talking to you. I don't get to do that much around here."

"You don't talk to your wife or my aunties?"

Rafik turned and faced her. "How old are you?"

"Eighteen." She added two years. It felt like the right thing to say.

"Good, you're almost an adult. Marriage, eh... With my wife, it's always I need money for this... or the house gossip. Maybe it's our fault, and I mean the men. Women just take care of us and the children, cook, gossip with friends and if they have a business they take care of it, and they are satisfied." He tapped her wrist.

"But auntie Fati has interesting, political conversations with men in the communications centre," Nana countered.

He was quiet and then said, "I know, but people say things about her, call her names just because she's independent and doing it on her own. This village thinking, eish my dear, you don't know how lucky you are."

"Then I can't imagine what people say about me."

"You're young so they won't worry your life. But when you're older... I know your grandmother doesn't like Fati talking to all those men. But enough about that." His hand moved down from her wrist to her thigh.

"Hmmm," Nana said. She couldn't tell whether that was a response to his hand or to the realisation that Auntie Fati, the only woman she'd want to emulate, was called names. It was his hand, she decided. She liked it there, and yet the moment felt wrong. A fly landed on her cheek, he rubbed the area with the thumb of his other hand.

She sighed and then silence fell. Rafik's hand still rested on her thigh, rubbing warm circles on her skin. She shuddered. This was new. The feelings she was experiencing.

"Don't forget me when you get back to the big city," he said and retracted his hand.

"Of course, I won't."

He laughed, and spit sprayed out of his mouth. "When you get back to your boyfriends, big TVs and cars you'll forget about your good friend Rafik. But that's life."

"I don't have boyfriends," she said quietly, took his hands and stared into his eyes. She didn't know why she'd taken his hands or what was making her so bold. "I will never forget you."

"That's what you say now, but we'll see." He stared back.

What is going to happen? She saw something flicker in Rafik's eyes. Like raw hunger, and it made her feel wanted and uncomfortable. She felt starved too. She turned her gaze away from his eyes and caught a flick of the silky lemon green of her grandmother's scarf behind the wall. She let go of Rafik's hands.

"Are you OK?"

"Yes, yes. I just forgot something." She sped into her grandmother's room, grabbed her book — *Tar Baby* — and lay on the bed, her heart pounding. She can't have seen, Nana prayed. Maybe she saw me run in, but not me and Rafik under the tree.

Sadiya wrapped her cloth around her flat chest and shook Nana awake, so they could start filling the water barrel. The taps flowed once a day, at 5 a.m. As the water gushed into a metal bucket, Nana adjusted her own cloth. She yawned loudly and stretched out.

"Nana, when you go back to Akarrra, I hope you won't forget me."

"I won't forget you."

"You will write me?"

"Of course, I will. But we still have plenty of time before I go back."

"Oh, grandmother didn't tell you?" Sadiya's muscles flexed as she lifted the heavy bucket.

"Tell me what?"

"Uncle Osman is going back to Accra in two days, so he's taking you with him."

"Nobody asks me anything." Nana folded her arms and stared at the water running in rivulets on Sadiya's arms.

"Grandmother knows what is best for you." She lowered her voice. "Uncle Rafik is a dangerous character. You have to be careful of him. Everybody sees how close the two of you are now." She pursed her lips and glanced furtively around.

"You're joking, right?" Nana's voice was higher than needed. She felt a little naked. That everyone knew about the two of them. That something beautiful that was blooming was rudely cut short.

Uncle Osman sat to her right, and this time, she had the window seat. She stared out the window. As the tears slid down her cheeks, she pictured Rafik's face. The tall grass, now blue in the moonlight, swayed gently. She had not really thought of what she would have done with Rafik. All she was sure of was that it would have been beautiful. She had never met any one like him, who'd told her she was smart and beautiful. She smiled through the tears. In a month, she would be back in class with idiotic boys whose aim in life was to get the latest Nike sneakers. The girls wanted their blue and white uniforms to be shorter and shorter, just for the boys. All she'd felt was his thumb on her cheek, his hand on her thigh and those intelligent eyes. He'd made her feel like a woman. She touched her cheek and kept looking at the tall, blue grass.

Tamale Blues

Ayesha Harruna Attah has worked as a freelance writer for media houses in Accra, the *AFRican Magazine* and *Yachting Magazine*. Born and raised in Ghana, Ayesha then moved to Massachusetts to study biochemistry at Mount Holyoke College. She holds an M.S. in magazine journalism from Columbia University and is now pursuing an MFA degree at NYU. *Harmattan Rain,* her first novel was short-listed for the Commonwealth Writers Prize in 2010. She loves fried plantain, hot days and beaches.